L O N E S T A

# The

Robert E. Hollmann

LONESTAR LEGENDS

presents

# *The Alamo*

by

ROBERT E. HOLLMANN

Printed in the United States of America.

For information address:
Lonestar Legends Publishing
620 N Grant, Ste 915
Odessa, TX 79761

Library of Congress Cataloging-in-Publication Data
Hollmann, Robert E., 1944 -

The Alamo / Robert E. Hollmann

Library of Congress Control Number: 2010936843
p. cm.

ISBN 1492286346

10 9 8 7 6 5 4 3 2 1

Visit our website at:
www.lonestarlegends.org

*Dedication*

*To the Defenders of the Alamo and my newest Granddaughter*
*Emmy Glen Hollmann*

Acknowledgements

As always, a lot of people gave support and encouragement for the writing of this book. My family is always supportive. My friends kept asking when the next book would be out. But the person I want to especially acknowledge is a third grade teacher at an elementary school in Odessa, Texas. Andria Millican is a special teacher, the kind we need more of. She read one of my books to her students, and when they asked how they could get one, she bought each of her students a copy. I believe that shows her love of teaching and for her students. I appreciate the fact that she is making reading important to her students. Andria Millican is truly an outstanding teacher. So, one more time, to my children, Rob, Kristina, and Kasey. To my grandchildren, who inspired me to write this series of books, Dylan, Addison, and Kirsten, and to my wife, Kathy, thank you for all you do.

*Robert E. Hollmann*
*Odessa, Texas*
*March 2009*

# The Alamo

# Chapter One

"Hurry up, students," Ms. Millican called to her junior high class. "The museum will be closing soon, and we still have a lot to see."

The students fell into a line behind Ms. Millican and followed her through the exhibits.

"Don't touch anything," a museum guard warned a student. "These exhibits are very old, and they break easily."

Jimmy Morgan pulled his hand away from the glass bowl he had been reaching for. He smiled at the guard and trailed along after the other students. He caught up with Nancy Riley and motioned for her to drop back to the end of the line of students. When they had reached the end of the line, Jimmy grabbed Nancy's hand, and they both stopped. "What do you want, Jimmy?" Nancy asked.

"This museum tour is boring. Sure, there's some neat stuff, but they won't let you touch it. Let's go find something else to do."

"We can't leave the class. If Ms. Millican finds out we left the class, we'll be in big trouble."

"She won't know we're gone. It's thirty minutes until the museum closes. We can find something fun to do and be back when they get ready to leave."

"Well…" Nancy looked around. The other class members were walking into another room. "What do you want to do?"

Jimmy looked around. "Look over there. There's a door. Let's see what's on the other side of it."

Nancy looked at the door. "That sign says 'stay out.' I think only people who work here can go in there."

"Yeah. Well, that's probably where they keep the really neat things. Come on. Nobody's looking. Let's just take a peek, and then we'll come right back out."

"I don't know, Jimmy. We could get in a lot of trouble. I think we should join the class," Nancy said.

"Well, go on. Join the class. I thought you were fun, Nancy. I thought you would like to see things the other class members didn't get to see. They don't put the best stuff out here. They keep it in other rooms so only they can see it. I'm going to go see what's behind that door. If you're afraid, go on and find Ms. Millican."

Jimmy walked toward the door. Nancy looked back at the room the class had walked into. She couldn't see anyone. There was no one else in the room but Jimmy and her.

Nancy took a deep breath and called out, "Wait for me, Jimmy."

"Not so loud," Jimmy said. "We don't want everybody coming with us."

Nancy and Jimmy walked up to the door. It was a metal door with no windows. Jimmy pushed gently on the door, but it did not move.

"It must be locked," Nancy said. "Come on, let's go."

Jimmy grabbed the doorknob and turned it. The door opened, and Jimmy smiled as he turned to Nancy.

"It's open. Come on. Let's get inside before somebody sees us."

Jimmy pushed the door open far enough for him to walk into the room. Nancy stood looking at the open door.

"Will you come on? Somebody's going to catch us if you don't hurry."

Nancy shook her head and sighed, then ran into the room. When Nancy was inside, Jimmy shut the door. He heard a click as the door slammed shut. The room was dark. The two students strained their eyes to see through the blackness.

"I bet there's a light switch somewhere," Jimmy said. "Come on, feel along the wall. It has to be right by the door."

Nancy and Jimmy placed their hands on the wall and moved them until Nancy found the switch. She pushed the switch up, and the room was filled with light. When their eyes became used to the light, the students looked around to see what was in the room.

In the middle of the room was a large table. A model of something filled nearly the whole table. A sign standing next to the table said, “Coming soon—an exhibit on the history of Texas.” Other tables held guns, swords, dishes, and many other objects that were going to be part of the exhibit.

In a corner of the room, a statue of a woman looked down on them. She was dressed in flowing robes and held a torch in her right hand. A sign beside the statue said “Lady Texas.”

Jimmy took a few steps toward the center of the room. Nancy grabbed his arm and pulled him back. “Come on. Let’s go. I really don’t think we should be here. We’re going to be in so much trouble when Ms. Millican finds out we’re gone.”

“Don’t be a scaredy-cat,” Jimmy said. “We’re already in. We might as well look around. There’s nobody here but that stupid-looking statue.”

Nancy looked at the statue. “I don’t think she’s stupid-looking. I think she’s really beautiful.”

“That old thing? Beautiful? Man, you need to get your eyes checked. I’ve seen prettier things thrown away. Let’s see what else is in here.”

The students walked around the room. They looked at the exhibits lying on the tables. Jimmy picked up some of the guns. “Wow, these are heavy. I’d sure hate to carry one of these around all day.”

Nancy picked up a bonnet and tried it on. “How do I look, Jimmy?” she asked.

"You look nearly as goofy as that statue. It's a good thing you didn't live back then and have to wear one of those."

"You're not being very nice," Nancy said. "I'm going to find the class."

Jimmy put down the sword he was holding. "Come on, Nancy. I was just kidding. You know I think you're pretty."

"Maybe so," Nancy said. "But I think we need to get back to Ms. Millican."

"Oh, all right. There's nothing in here that interesting anyway. I don't want to waste my time on an exhibit about Texas history. We get enough of that boring stuff in school."

Jimmy and Nancy walked over to the door. Jimmy grabbed the doorknob and turned it. He pushed the door, but it didn't budge.

"Stop playing around, Jimmy. It's getting late. We need to find the class."

"I'm not playing," Jimmy said. "The door's locked. We can't get out."

# Chapter Two

"What do you mean, we can't get out? Open this door, Jimmy. This isn't funny," Nancy said.

Jimmy pulled harder on the door. "It really won't open. Here, try it for yourself."

Jimmy stepped back and watched as Nancy grabbed the doorknob. She pulled as hard as she could, but the door would not budge.

Nancy began to pound on the door with her fists. "Let us out. Somebody let us out!" she yelled.

"No one can hear you, my dear," a voice said.

"What did you say?" Nancy asked Jimmy.

"I didn't say anything," Jimmy said. "But I heard it too. There must be somebody else in here with us."

Jimmy and Nancy slowly turned around. They looked around the room but didn't see anyone.

"I wonder who said that," Jimmy said.

"I did," the voice answered.

"I heard that," Nancy said. "And I know neither one of us said anything."

She turned and tried to open the door again. "Somebody let us out. We're locked in this room," she called.

"I told you, no one can hear you," the voice said. "All you're doing is making an awful racket."

Jimmy walked over to a table and picked up an old sword. "Whoever you are, you better leave us alone," he said. "I have a sword, and I'll use it if I have to."

"Oh, pooh," said the voice. "Put the sword down. You'll probably cut an ear off. I'm not going to hurt you."

"Yeah, well, if you're not a bad guy, show us who you are," Jimmy said.

"All right, here I come."

Nancy and Jimmy looked around the room. They didn't see anyone. Suddenly, a light began to glow around the statue of Lady Texas. The children shielded their eyes from the bright glow. The light began to fade, and then Lady Texas stepped down from the pedestal she had been standing on. The children looked at her in disbelief. Lady Texas was no longer a stone statue; she was a beautiful woman. She smiled as she walked toward the two children.

"I'm sorry if I scared you," she said. "I'm Lady Texas."

The sword fell from Jimmy's hand and made a great clattering noise as it hit the floor. Nancy stared wide-eyed at the figure walking toward them. She backed up until she hit the wall and could go no further. She reached behind her for the doorknob, but was unable to find it.

"Don't bother with the door. It's locked, as I said. Please don't be afraid. I won't hurt you. Why don't you tell me your names?" Lady Texas said.

Nancy looked Lady Texas. "My name is Nancy. This is Jimmy. Our class was on a tour of the museum, and we came in here to see what was in this room. We don't mean any harm. We just want to leave and go find our class."

Lady Texas smiled. "Oh, your class left hours ago. You've been here longer than you think. The museum is closed until tomorrow. There is a night watchman, but he's probably asleep at the front desk by now. I'm afraid you're in here for the night." Lady Texas turned to Jimmy. "Well, Jimmy, do you still think I'm ugly?"

Jimmy swallowed hard. "No, Lady Texas. I was just making a joke. I make jokes all the time. Just ask Nancy. I'm always making jokes, aren't I? Why, I think you're real pretty."

"Why, thank you, Jimmy. That was nice of you to say. Well, what do you two think of the new exhibit?"

"I'm sure it'll be nice when it's finished," Nancy said.

"What about you, Jimmy? Do you like it? I heard you say it was boring," Lady Texas said.

Jimmy looked at Lady Texas and then looked around the room. "Well, I didn't mean just this stuff. I think history is boring. It is just dates and talking about dead people."

Lady Texas smiled. "No, Jimmy. History is more than just dates. And the people were alive at one time. Just like you are now. When you study history, you study about those people and their lives. It is really very interesting."

"If you say so," Jimmy said.

"Come on. Let me show you how interesting history can be." Lady Texas walked over to the table with the model sitting on it. Nancy and Jimmy followed her.

"Now see this model? One of the most famous events in Texas history took place here."

"Are you kidding?" Jimmy asked. "That's just an old rundown building. I bet it doesn't even have a name."

"Oh, yes it does," Lady Texas said. "Its name is the Alamo."

"Now, I know you're trying to fool us. This doesn't look anything like the Alamo. Right, Nancy?"

"That's right. My parents took me to see the Alamo once, and I've seen a lot of pictures of it. This building doesn't even have a roof."

"The Alamo you see today is very different from the Alamo in 1836. There have been many changes, including adding a roof."

Jimmy looked at the model. "This doesn't even look like a fort. I know there was a big battle at the Alamo. There had to be a real fort to have such a big battle."

"Oh, there was a big battle there, all right. Would you like me to tell you about it? Or better yet, why don't we go see it?"

Nancy shook her head. "I don't know. My mother is probably worried about me. I better be getting home."

"I told you, it will be tomorrow before anyone finds you. We will be back by then. What do you say? Want to see the story of the Alamo?"

Jimmy nodded. "That would be fun. But I don't want to get shot."

Lady Texas smiled. "Oh, don't worry. No one will be able to see or hear us. We'll just watch and listen to the people who were part of the story of the Alamo."

Nancy shrugged. "How do we get there?"

"That's easy," Lady Texas said. "Each of you take one of my hands. Hold on tight and don't let go."

Jimmy and Nancy walked over to Lady Texas and took her hands. They squeezed them tightly. A mist began to rise and curl around them. It got thicker and thicker until they could see nothing but the mist. They heard the sound of the wind, and it felt like they were flying.

"Hold on tight," Lady Texas said. "Next stop, the Alamo."

# Chapter Three

THE MIST SWIRLED AROUND THE CHILDREN as they flew through it. Nancy closed her eyes and squeezed Lady Texas's hand. Jimmy looked around, trying to see through the cloudy mist. He felt his hand slipping and gripped Lady Texas harder.

Slowly the mist began to dissolve. The children were standing next to Lady Texas, looking at a barren landscape. A town with adobe buildings lay just in front of them.

As Jimmy became accustomed to the sight, he looked up at Lady Texas and said, "Wow, that was cool. Where are we?"

"We are looking at the town of San Antonio de Bexar."

"What?" Jimmy said. "I've been to San Antonio. It didn't look like this. It had big buildings. What is this place, really?"

Lady Texas smiled. "Really, this is San Antonio. It is San Antonio in 1836. As you can see, things were quite different back then."

"Where's the Alamo?" Nancy asked.

Lady Texas pointed to a rundown set of buildings. "Right over there. It's a little bit outside of town."

"No," Jimmy said. "The Alamo was a fort. That doesn't look like a fort to me."

"You see, Jimmy, the Alamo wasn't built to be a fort. The Alamo was founded in 1724 by Spanish missionaries who came here to teach the Indians about Christianity. They called their mission San Antonio de Valero."

Nancy frowned. "If they called it that, why is it named the Alamo today?"

Lady Texas looked at the old mission. "There are two stories about that. One says the mission was called the Alamo after a company of cavalry from Los Alamos de Parras. The other story says it was called the Alamo because of the cottonwood trees that grow close by. 'Alamo' in Spanish means cottonwood."

"Can we go down and get a closer look?" Jimmy asked.

"Of course. Follow me."

Lady Texas led the children along a dusty road and through the gates of the Alamo. Inside, men were working to turn the old mission into a fort. Some men were building a wooden fence along one side of the Alamo to close a gap between the fence and the chapel. Other men were lifting cannons onto the walls. They stopped and watched as a large cannon was placed facing the town.

A man walked up to the group who had just placed the cannon on the wall. "Good job, men. That cannon will help a lot when Santa Anna's army gets here."

One of the men took off his hat and wiped his forehead. "When do you think he'll get here, Colonel Travis?"

Colonel Travis looked out over the wall. "Well, Captain Dickinson, according to Juan Seguin's scouts, Santa Anna is on his way here right now. Anybody with any sense knows that can't be true. You can't move an army in the dead of winter across a desert. There's nothing for the horses to eat. I don't think he'll be here until next spring. That should give us plenty of time to get this old mission in shape. It will also allow time for other men to join us. As you know, we need more men."

Captain Dickinson leaned against the cannon. "Jim Bowie believes Seguin's scouts. He says we should be ready real soon."

Travis shook his head. "I'm afraid Bowie has been fooled by the reports. But he is not a real military man. He doesn't understand how hard it would be to move a large army from Mexico to San Antonio in the winter. No, I don't think Santa Anna will be here for several months. Well, you men better get back to work. We need to be ready whenever Santa Anna gets here."

Travis walked away as the men began stacking cannonballs next to the cannon. Jimmy watched Travis walk across the plaza of the Alamo. "Was that really William Travis? I remember reading about him in our textbook."

“I remember too,” Nancy said. “And Jim Bowie’s here. Will we see him too?”

Lady Texas smiled. “Yes, you’ll see him and many more before our journey’s through. Are you bored, Jimmy? Do you want to go back?”

Jimmy shook his head. “No. This is fun. I want to see more.”

“Well, come along. Let’s go into town.”

They walked down the dusty streets of San Antonio. The sound of a guitar and laughter came out of one of the buildings. A woman walked out of the general store carrying a package in her arms. She headed toward a house at the end of the street.

“Let’s follow her,” Lady Texas said.

The children walked beside Lady Texas as she followed the woman into her house. The lady set her package down and walked over and put an apron over her dress.

“Hello, Susannah,” a man said as he walked through the door. “Are you going to make one of your famous pies?”

“Hello, Juan,” Susannah said. “Yes, I just bought some nice juicy apples at the store. It should be ready tonight. Will you be here for supper?”

“You bet,” Juan said. “I’m not going to tell the others about the pie, either. Maybe some of them won’t be here if they don’t know you’re making a pie. Well, I better be going. There’s a lot of work to do at the Alamo.”

“Juan, if you see Almeron, tell him to be home on time tonight. He spends so much time at the Alamo, he might as well move there.”

"All right, but if he's late, I get his piece of pie."

Juan left, and Susannah began getting her pie ready. She heard a knock at the door, and she looked up to see a tall man in a fringed jacket standing there.

"Pardon me, ma'am," he said. "Would you be the owner of this fine establishment?"

Susannah wiped her hands on her apron and pushed a lock of hair out of her face. "Why, yes. My name is Susannah Dickinson."

The man walked in and smiled. "Nice to meet you, Mrs. Dickinson. My name is David Crockett."

# Chapter Four

"I know who Davy Crockett is," Nancy said. "I remember studying about him. I can't believe that's really him."

"Yes, Nancy," Lady Texas said. "That is really Davy Crockett. You are going to see many famous people before this story is over."

Susannah Dickinson held out her hand. "Nice to meet you, Mr. Crockett. My name is Susannah Dickinson. This is my boarding house."

Davy shook Susannah's hand. "Nice to meet you too, Mrs. Dickinson. But please call me David. Or Davy, if you believe the stories. Mr. Crockett is my father. It makes me feel old for people to call me that."

"All right, Davy. And you must call me Susannah. Now what can I do for you?"

"Well, I just ran into a fellow named Juan Seguin. He says you run the best boarding house and cook the best meals of anybody in San Antonio. I sure would like to sleep in a bed for a change, and home cooking sounds mighty good to me right now."

"I just happen to have an empty bed, Davy. You're welcome to it. Supper will be ready around six. I haven't fixed anything special. But there should be plenty."

"Sounds good to me. Say, did I tell you how I came by this fine cap? Of course not. I just met you. Well, it seems one day I was out hunting, and as I was walking through the woods I looked up and saw a fat old raccoon sitting in a tree. I thought, 'That old raccoon would make a real fine cap, and I sure do need a new one.' So I pointed my gun at the raccoon, but before I could pull the trigger, he raised his hands and said, 'Don't shoot, Davy. I'll come on down.' Well, that raccoon crawled down out of that tree and crawled right into my bag. And he did make a fine cap, as you can see."

"That's quite a story, Davy," Susannah said.

"Oh, I have a bunch more," Davy said.

"I certainly look forward to hearing them. Well, I better get busy if you want supper tonight."

"I need to find Colonel Travis. Do you know where he might be?"

"I haven't seen him today. He's usually at the Alamo. If you go over there, be sure to say hello to my husband, Almeron. He'll be glad to meet you, especially since we're from Tennessee too."

"I'll be sure and look him up. Goodbye, Susannah. I look forward to suppertime."

Lady Texas watched Davy walk out the door. "Come on, kids. Let's go see what's going on at the Alamo."

Soon they were back inside the old mission. The men were working harder than before. They were walking around the plaza, when suddenly they heard loud voices coming from a room. They went into the room and saw Travis talking to Jim Bowie and Juan Seguin.

Jim Bowie was mad. He pounded on the table as he said, "Why don't you believe the scouts? They are risking their lives to bring you information about Santa Anna's army. They have no reason to lie to you. They have chosen to fight with us. I don't understand you."

"I would expect you to side with Juan in this matter. However, as the commander of this fort, I must make my decisions based on more than the word of some scout that I don't know."

Bowie looked at Travis. "Who said you were in command here?"

Travis took a deep breath, then looked at the two men standing in front of him. "Colonel Neil left me in command when he left to go home. He said I was to be in charge until he returned."

"He did, did he?" Bowie coughed, then sat down. "Well, we'll see what the men say about that."

"What do you mean?" Travis asked.

"We'll have an election. The men can choose their leader."

"Fine," Travis said. "When we finish the work this evening, we'll have the election."

A knock on the door caused the men to stop their argument. They looked at the door to see Davy Crockett standing there.

"Sorry to bother you," Davy said. "I just rode in with my men, and I was wondering if there's something we can do? My name's David Crockett."

"Davy Crockett," Travis said. "From Tennessee? Congressman Crockett?"

Davy smiled. "It's not Congressman anymore. Seems like in the last election the folks back home wanted somebody else, so they voted me out. I decided to see what Texas looked like, so here I am."

Jim Bowie walked over and shook his hand. "We're glad you're here, Davy. Have you found a place to stay?"

"I just signed on over at Susannah Dickinson's boarding house. I think that will do me fine."

"Yes, that's the best place in town, and Susannah's a fine lady," Bowie said.

Travis stood up. "Come on, Davy, let me show you around the Alamo. Bowie, Seguin, we can finish our discussion later."

Travis and Davy walked out the door. Bowie and Seguin followed them.

"Lady Texas," Nancy said, "Why are Bowie and Travis fighting? If Santa Anna's on his way, they should be working together."

Lady Texas smiled. "You're right, Nancy. They should be working together. Unfortunately, they don't like each other, and that makes it hard for them to agree on things. Well, come on. We have a long way to go."

Jimmy took Lady Texas's hand. "Where are we going?" he asked.

"Why, we're going to find Santa Anna's army," she said.

# Chapter Five

"Look at all those soldiers," Jimmy whispered.

The two students and Lady Texas stood on a little hill and watched Santa Anna's army cross the Rio Grande River. Lady Texas smiled at Jimmy. "You don't have to whisper. They can't see you or hear you."

"Oh, yeah. It's just that there are so many soldiers it scares me. How many do you think there are?"

Nancy started to count, but soon gave up. "I don't know, but I bet there are a couple of thousand at least. It looks like Juan's scouts were telling the truth. Travis had better start listening to them."

Some of the soldiers had crossed the river and were trying to dry their wet uniforms. They all came to attention as a man in a bright uniform rode his prancing horse past them.

"Do you see that man?" Lady Texas asked, pointing to the man riding the horse. The children nodded. "That's Santa Anna. He's the president of Mexico, and he is also the general in command of this army. He has decided to drive the Texans out of San Antonio and then out of Texas."

"Lady Texas," Nancy said, "there aren't nearly enough men in San Antonio to fight this army. Surely they will leave before Santa Anna gets there."

"No, they won't," Lady Texas said. "The men in San Antonio believe they must stop Santa Anna there. They believe that is where they must make their stand."

"Look over there." Jimmy pointed to a man sitting on a horse on another small hill. "What's he doing?"

"That is one of Juan Seguin's scouts. He's counting Santa Anna's soldiers. He'll be taking a message back to San Antonio soon."

Before long, the man turned his horse and rode away from the enemy army. The children watched him ride away. "I hope Travis believes him when he tells him how many soldiers are coming," Jimmy said.

Nancy nodded as she watched the last enemy soldiers walk out of the river. "Me too. Lady Texas, is there any way we can tell Colonel Travis about the enemy army?"

Lady Texas shook her head. "No. We are here to watch history. I'm afraid we can't change it. Come on now. Let's go back to San Antonio."

Back in San Antonio the men were walking out of the Alamo after a hard day's work. They walked into town and gathered around the plaza. Soon, a large crowd of men had gathered. They were waiting to vote for their leader. Soon, Travis and Bowie arrived. They walked to the front of the gathered men and stood on a bench so they could be seen. Jim Bowie took off his hat and waved it. The men quit talking and looked at Bowie.

"All right. You know why we're here. Colonel Neil has been called home. We need someone to be in charge until he gets back. Unless somebody else wants the job, you will vote for either me or Colonel Travis. All right. All who want Colonel Travis, raise your hands."

Nancy and Jimmy looked at the crowd of men. Only a few raised their hands.

"Now if you want me to be your leader," Bowie said, "raise your hands."

Nearly everybody in the crowd raised his hand. Bowie had easily won the election. Bowie turned to Travis. "Well, the men voted. Looks like I won."

Travis shook his head. "You aren't a regular army officer. You are a volunteer. I still command the regular troops. You command the volunteers."

Bowie shook his head. "You're a bad loser, Travis. It doesn't matter, though. Most of the men are volunteers. Come on, Juan, let's go see if Susannah has supper ready."

The crowd broke up as men went to their homes. Soon, Travis was standing by himself in the middle of the plaza.

"I feel sorry for him," Nancy said.

"Bowie is more popular with the men, but Travis is a brave man. He will have a big part to play in the story of Texas," Lady Texas said.

It was dark in the plaza now. Lights shone from the windows of a few houses. They could hear a guitar playing and the sound of laughter. In one of the houses, a woman was singing her baby to sleep. Travis stood in the plaza and looked around. A dog ran by trying to find some food. Out on the prairie a coyote howled, and in the distance another answered it.

Finally, Travis turned and walked away toward his house. The plaza lay empty under the full moon, while not too far away, Santa Anna's army lay down to get some rest before continuing their journey to San Antonio the next day.

# CHAPTER SIX

THE NEXT DAY, THE CHILDREN AND Lady Texas walked to the Alamo. As they entered the courtyard, Jimmy turned to Nancy. "Why do you want to come here and see Travis?"

"I'm worried about him," Nancy said. "He seemed so sad last night after he lost the election. I just want to make sure he's all right."

"What can you do if he's not?" Jimmy asked.

"Jimmy, Nancy is a kind person. She doesn't like to see people hurt. I think it's nice she wants to check on Colonel Travis."

"Well, I'd rather be doing something else, like listening to Davy Crockett tell stories."

Lady Texas led the way into Travis's room. "We can hear his stories later. He never runs out of them."

Travis was sitting at a small desk writing a letter. He looked up as a young man entered. "Good morning, Bill," he said.

"James Bonham." Travis smiled as he stood and held out his hand. "When did you get back?"

"I got in late last night. I finished my business in San Felipe and decided I might as well come back here."

"Well, it's good to have you back here. We sure can use more men. Especially good ones."

"How are you this morning? I heard about the election," Bonham said.

"Oh, don't worry about that. I'm fine. I didn't expect those men to vote for me. They're all Bowie's friends."

"Bill, I've known you since we were kids in South Carolina. I can tell when something's bothering you."

Travis shook his head. "We have more serious problems to worry about than an election. Juan Seguin's scouts keep reporting Santa Anna's army is getting nearer. I don't believe he's coming now, but he will be here one day. Look around. We don't have nearly enough men to repair this old mission, let alone defend it. If we don't get reinforcements soon, it won't matter when Santa Anna gets here. We won't be able to stop him."

"There's a convention meeting at Washington on the Brazos. Have you asked them to send you some men?"

"I don't think they have the power to do that. The governor and the legislature are fighting each other. I don't really know who to send a message to."

Bonham took off his hat and rubbed his head. "What about Sam Houston? Ask him to raise some troops and come here."

"A man came to town yesterday. He said Houston had gone off to make some treaties with the Indians. I'm writing a letter now to Colonel Fannin at Goliad. Maybe he can send us some men. Come on, Jim. Let's take a walk around and see how the repairs are coming."

Travis and Bonham walked out the door. They stood for a minute and watched the work going on all around them. They walked over to where two young men were piling dirt against a wall. "Pile that dirt high, boys. We need to reinforce that wall. Jim, I want you to meet two of our best men. This is Daniel William Cloud and James Rose."

Bonham stepped forward and shook the young men's hands. "Glad to meet you. Looks like you got a big job to do."

Daniel Cloud took off his hat and wiped the sweat from his face. "Yeah, it's a big job, and it seems like it never ends."

James Rose took a drink of water. "I thought I was coming to Texas to fight, but it seems like I came here to put Texas in a big pile."

"When Santa Anna's army gets here, you'll be glad for every foot of this dirt. The more dirt you pile up, the more cannonballs you'll stop."

Travis looked at an old man who was sitting down with his back against the wall. His head was resting on his chest, and they could hear his snores.

"Who's that?" Bonham asked.

"His name is Louis Moses Rose," Travis said. "He came in with Bowie."

Travis turned to the two young men. "What's the matter with Rose?"

Daniel Cloud shook his head. "I don't think anything is wrong with him. He said he was tired of working and just walked over and went to sleep."

James Rose threw a shovelful of dirt on the pile. "He's not much good when he does do some work," he said. "Might just as well let him sleep."

"We don't have enough men to let some of them sleep all day," Travis said as he walked over and kicked the bottom of Rose's boot. "Wake up," Travis said.

Rose jerked awake. "Who's kicking me?" he angrily asked.

"I am," Travis said. "We need men working, not sitting around doing nothing. We have to get the Alamo ready before the enemy army gets here."

"Well, get it ready without me," Rose said as he turned on his side.

"Get up now, and go to work," Travis said.

Rose got slowly to his feet. "Jim Bowie tells me what to do, not you," he said.

"Bowie's not here, and I'm telling you to go to work. Right now," Travis said. He took a shovel from Daniel Cloud and held it toward Rose. "Now take this shovel and get to work."

Rose took the shovel from Travis and began to throw small shovelfuls of dirt against the wall. Travis watched him work for a while, then he and Bonham walked off.

"What do you think, Jim?" Travis asked. "Can we beat Santa Anna's army with men like Moses Rose?"

Bonham looked back at Rose, who had already given the shovel back to Daniel Cloud and sat down and leaned against the wall. "Think you better pray more men get here real soon. A lot more of them, too."

# Chapter Seven

"Susannah, did I ever tell you about the time I tried to grin down a bear?"

The children and Lady Texas watched as Davy Crockett talked to Susannah Dickinson.

"Why, no, Davy," Susannah said. "I don't believe you did."

"Well, one day I was out hunting. It started to rain, so I sat down under a tree. Some rain got on my powder, and I had to wait for it to dry out before I could shoot it. So, while I'm sitting there, all of a sudden I see this big old bear walking toward me. My powder was still wet, so I couldn't shoot him. I just watched him getting nearer and nearer."

"Oh my goodness," Susannah said. "What did you do, Davy?"

"Well, that bear stops right in front of me. He stands up on his hind legs and lets out a big old growl. I thought for a minute, and then I stood up and looked that bear right in the eye and started to grin at him."

Susannah shook her head. "You grinned at the bear?"

"Yes, I did. It seems to me that it's hard to eat somebody if they're grinning at you. So that bear, he drops down to four legs and looks at me all puzzled like. I keep grinning, but after a while, my face gets tired. So, I stop grinning at the bear.

"Well, when I stop grinning, the bear stands back up, growls, and takes a swipe at me with one of his big old paws. I turn around and commence to running as fast as I can toward my house. I could hear the bear running behind me. I could feel his breath on my neck. I want to tell you a bear's breath didn't smell too good.

"I never ran so fast in my whole life. The bear kept falling further and further behind. Soon, he stopped, and I ran until I got to my house. I ran inside and bolted the door. I was shaking all over. After a while, I looked out the window and that bear was still standing there looking at my house. Finally, he turned and walked away. I never tried to grin down a bear again. I tried it on some rabbits and squirrels, but it hasn't worked yet."

"Maybe you can grin Santa Anna back to Mexico."

Davy and Susannah turned to see Jim Bowie and Juan Seguin standing in the doorway.

"Hello, Jim," Davy said. "I didn't know you had come in."

"We've been standing here for a while. I didn't want to stop such a good story."

"Any more news on Santa Anna's army?" Susannah asked.

"One of my men just came in," Juan said. "Several days ago he saw Santa Anna's army crossing the Rio Grande."

"Those are the soldiers we saw," Jimmy said.

"Yes," Nancy said. "Juan's scout must have been the man we saw."

Juan sat down at the table. "My man said there were several thousand men. They also had many cannons. If they were on the Rio Grande a couple of days ago, they will be here soon."

"More news of the ghost army?" Travis and Bonham entered the room. "Don't you get tired of spreading these stories?"

Nancy yelled at Travis. "They're not stories. They're true. We saw them too."

"Yes, we did," Jimmy said. "There are thousands of them."

Travis smiled. "If that report is true, and I don't believe it is, we better get the Alamo finished so we'll be ready when Santa Anna gets here."

Davy looked around the room. "I'm new here, so I don't know what all's gone on, but it seems to me that Texas is an awfully big place. Why is everybody so all-fired ready to lock themselves up in a rundown old mission when there's miles of prairie out there? Why don't we have Santa Anna chase us and we can attack him when we want to?"

"Davy, one of the things we do agree on is that here is where we need to stop Santa Anna's army. We can't let him advance into our settlements. Why, Bowie had orders from Houston himself to blow up the Alamo and leave here. But, as I said, we all agree that we must stand and fight here."

Crockett turned to Bowie. "Houston told you to blow up the Alamo and you didn't do it?"

Bowie smiled. "Yeah. I guess old Sam'll be madder than a wet hen when he gets back and finds I didn't do what he told me to. But by then we'll have whipped Santa Anna and sent him back to Mexico with his tail between his legs, so there won't be much he can do about it."

Davy shook his head. "Maybe so, but it seems to me that it's a lot harder to hunt a bear in a forest than to hunt one holed up in a cave. Somehow I get the feeling that when we get inside the Alamo, I'm going to feel like a bear in a cave."

Travis turned to Bowie. "Let's go to my office and talk about this new report. By the way, Bowie, you need to talk to some of your men. They don't want to do any work around the Alamo. We need everyone working if we are going to have any chance of being ready for Santa Anna."

"Who are you talking about?" Bowie asked.

"Well, the latest is Moses Rose. He was sleeping, and I woke him up and told him to get to work. He said he only took orders from you. So, for all our sakes, you better give these men the order to work."

"I'll check on it," Bowie said as he and Seguin followed Travis and Bonham outside.

Davy watched them go. "I tell you, Susannah, I'm starting to get a bad feeling about this. Everyone needs to be working together, or we are going to have big problems. Well, right now my problem is that my plate's empty. How 'bout some more of your pie?"

# Chapter Eight

"Lady Texas," Nancy said as they walked through the Alamo courtyard, "just look around. There's no way the Texans can get this old mission ready to fight all those soldiers we saw."

"That's right," Jimmy said. "Look at that north wall. It's almost in ruins. They've made some repairs, but they can't keep out that many men. Then look over there. Between the chapel and that wall is a gap. I see them putting up a stockade, but that's not going to stop a full-scale attack."

Nancy pointed to the chapel roof as they walked inside. "Look up. There's not even a roof on the chapel.

Isn't there some way we can tell these men they need to leave?"

Lady Texas smiled and shook her head. "No. I told you, we can't change history. These men are here because they choose to be here. No one is making them stay. They are fighting for something they believe in, something so important to them that they are willing to die for it if they have to."

Jimmy looked around the Alamo. "I have a hard time believing that this old mission is worth dying for," he said.

"Me too," Nancy said. "Don't these men have families that they should be worrying about?"

"Yes, some of these men have families. And what they believe in is not this old mission. What they believe in is a dream they all share. A place where they can bring their families and start a new life. A place where their families can live free from unjust laws and bad rulers. What they are fighting for is what all men want for their families. For these men, this place is Texas. If they can beat Santa Anna's army, then Texas will be free, and their families can live in the way that these men dream of. These men are willing to fight and die if need be, not for the Alamo, but for Texas."

The children watched as some men rolled a cannon up a dirt ramp that went up to the top of the chapel. The cannon was placed on a platform that allowed it to shoot over the top of the roofless church. Two men stayed and stacked cannonballs next to the cannon as the other men walked down the ramp to get another cannon.

Lady Texas pointed to the two men on top of the platform. "See those two men? That's Almeron Dickinson and Gregorio Esparza. They both have wives and children. Susannah, the lady who has the boarding house, is married to Almeron. They have a little daughter, Angelina. Gregorio is married to Ana. They have four children. One of them is named Francisco, after Gregorio's brother. His brother is in Santa Anna's army. He is coming to fight the Texans and Gregorio."

"That's so sad," Nancy said. "I feel so sorry for these men."

Lady Texas smiled. "Don't feel sorry for them. They are making their own choice. They choose to stay and fight. Come on, let's go outside."

The activity in the Alamo courtyard had increased. Men were piling dirt up behind the north wall. Some others were digging a well. One man was playing some bagpipes as he looked over the wall at the empty prairie.

The children followed Lady Texas as she walked into Travis's office. He was talking to Bowie and Juan Seguin. "All right, I'll agree that maybe Santa Anna will be here sooner than I think. But there's nothing I can do about it."

Bowie leaned on the small desk. "Send out some patrols. Let them find out where that army is. Then we'll at least know how much time we'll have until they get here."

"We don't have enough men to send out patrols. You know how many we have. Not enough to finish the work we need to do here. I tell you what. We can place a sentry in the bell tower of San Fernando Church. That is high enough to give him a good view of the prairie for miles. If Santa Anna shows up, he can ring the bell. That should give us plenty of time to get into the Alamo."

Bowie turned to Seguin. "What do you think, Juan?"

Seguin shook his head. "I don't think it's the best idea, but Colonel Travis is right. We don't have enough men to send out patrols. It's important that we get the Alamo ready. To do that, we need as many men as possible working. So I guess putting a sentry in the bell tower is the best we can do for now. At least we will have some warning."

"All right, Travis. Let's find somebody and put him up there," Bowie said. He began to cough and had to sit down in a chair.

"Are you all right, Bowie?" Travis asked. "That cough doesn't sound too good."

Bowie waved a hand at Travis and finally caught his breath. "I'm fine. I have a cold that I can't seem to get rid of."

"Have you seen a doctor?" Travis asked.

Bowie nodded. "Yes. He said he wasn't sure what it was. He gave me some medicine, but so far it hasn't helped."

"Well, take care of yourself. We can't afford to lose any men. Especially men like you. I know we don't always agree, but you are a very good fighting man, and we need good fighting men." Travis stood up. "Oh, yes. Since today is George Washington's birthday, I think it would be a good idea to have a little party tonight. The men have been working hard, and I think a little fun would be good for them."

"I agree. I think we could all stand a little fun," Bowie said. "Come on, Juan. Let's go get things ready for the party."

While the Texans worked on the Alamo and planned their party, Santa Anna's army was camped not far away. Santa Anna called his cavalry commander into his tent. "General Sesma, I want you to take your cavalry and move on ahead. I think if we move fast enough, we can attack the Texans before they know we are here. I want you to attack San Antonio tonight."

# CHAPTER NINE

"COME ON, LADY TEXAS." NANCY GRABBED Lady Texas and tried to drag her to the plaza. "The party will be starting soon. I don't want to miss it. There has been so much worry about fighting, I'm ready for some fun."

"We have plenty of time. It's not even dark yet. Let's go over to the boarding house and see what's going on. I promise you, you won't miss the party."

In the boarding house, Susannah and Almeron Dickinson were having a talk. It was plain that they were not agreeing.

"All I'm saying, Almeron, is that I think we should get Angelina and leave now. Before it's too late. You've heard the stories. Santa Anna's coming, and his army is way too big for these few men to stop."

"Susannah, I've been trying for weeks to get you to leave. I agree. You and Angelina need to get out of here right now. I don't know when Santa Anna's army will get here. I think it will be sooner than we expect. But when it does get here, there will be a big fight. This will be no place for you and Angelina."

"Almeron, don't be telling me where my place is," Susannah said. "I know exactly where my place is. It's with you, wherever you are. We're a family, remember? We should be together in good times and bad. I'm not going to run away just because there might be danger. What I'm saying is, we should all go. As a family."

Almeron shook his head. "Susannah, I can't leave these men. We have all decided that this is where we must make our stand. This is where we must stop Santa Anna. I'm not the only person with a family. Many of these men have families, and they love them just as much as I love you. We want to make a home for them here, in Texas. A place where they can live safe and free and happy. That won't happen if men like Santa Anna are allowed to rule over us. That's why we will stop him. Right here. Whenever he shows up."

Susannah sat at the table. She stared silently at the floor. Finally she looked up. "All right, Almeron. If this town, if this rundown old mission is so important to you and to these other men, then it is important to me. I'll stay with you and see this through. We'll do it as a family."

"I don't want you to stay, Susannah. I want you to go where it's safe. After we've beaten Santa Anna, I'll come for you, and we'll make that happy home we both want.

But there is too much danger here for you and Angelina to stay."

"No, Almeron." Susannah stood up. "We won't leave you. If you stay, we stay. You'd better accept that."

Almeron sighed. "I don't want to talk about this anymore. We'll figure something out later. Come on, let's go to the party. We could use some fun."

"Can we go to the party now?" Nancy asked.

Lady Texas smiled. "All right. I think it's time to go."

The plaza was full of life. Lanterns were hung from the trees to give light. Tables were piled high with all sorts of tasty food. A small band was playing, and some people were dancing to the songs. People kept arriving, and soon the plaza was full. Jim Bowie, Juan Seguin, and several other men sat at a table quietly talking. William Travis sat at a table with James Bonham watching the people dance. Davy Crockett got his fiddle and joined the band in playing some lively tunes. Everyone was having a good time.

While the party was going on, a rider came into town. He found Bowie and Seguin and spoke quietly to them. When he had finished speaking, Bowie and Seguin walked over to Travis's table.

"Hello," Travis said. "Are you having a good time?"

Bowie looked around to make sure no one was listening, then said, "We were, until Juan's scout rode in. He has seen Santa Anna's army, and it's a lot closer than we thought. They should be here tomorrow. He said the cavalry left and he thinks they might attack tonight."

Travis sat silently for a few minutes. "I don't think it's likely they would try a cavalry attack in the dark. There are too many things that could go wrong. If they did attack, I believe we could hold them off, because it would be hard for cavalry to attack in a town. If Santa Anna's near, I think he'll attack in daylight, with his whole army. Let's let the men have a good time tonight. We have that sentry in the bell tower. He should see them coming far enough away to give us time to move into the Alamo."

Bowie looked at Seguin. "I think Travis is right. I don't think there will be an attack tonight. Tomorrow we can go look for ourselves. If the enemy is really here, we will find him."

"All right," Seguin said. "But I feel sure that tomorrow we'll find that army not far from here."

The party lasted until the wee hours of the morning. Finally, everyone went home, and the plaza was silent. The sun began to peek over the horizon, and the sentry in the bell tower rubbed his eyes as he thought about all the fun that he'd had at the party the night before.

Suddenly, he stopped rubbing his eyes and stared into the dim morning light. He looked once more, then ran to the bell rope and began to ring the bell.

Sleepy men stumbled from their rooms and ran toward the bell tower. Travis stopped at the foot of the tower and called up to the sentry. "Why are you ringing that bell?"

The sentry leaned out of the tower and pointed to the prairie. "The enemy is in view!" he said.

# Chapter Ten

THE CHILDREN AND LADY TEXAS WATCHED as the Texans ran from their rooms, rubbing the sleep from their eyes. Travis held his sword in his hand as he raced up the stairs to the bell tower. Bowie and Crockett were close behind him. Travis ran onto the tower platform and yelled at the sentry. "Why are you ringing that bell?"

"The enemy army is here," the sentry said.

Bowie looked at the prairie. "Where?" he asked.

"Right out there." The sentry turned and pointed to the prairie. Then he stopped, as he saw the prairie was empty. There was no enemy army in sight. "They were right out there a few minutes ago," he said. "Hundreds of them. Fancy uniforms and horses. I tell you, I saw them."

Travis, Bowie, and Crockett looked at the empty prairie once more. "You were probably dreaming about the party last night," Travis said. "Stay awake and don't ring that bell unless there is really something out there."

The three men walked down from the tower as the sentry gazed out onto the prairie once more. When they reached the bottom of the stairs, Travis stopped and looked up at the sentry. "He might have seen something. He's a good man. We probably need to send some men out there to check out the report."

"I'll be glad to go," Crockett said. "I've been in this town long enough. I could use some wide open spaces."

Bowie shook his head. "Davy, I know you're a great scout, but you're not real familiar with this country. I think we need to find some other people who are more familiar with the land to go look."

Travis nodded. "I agree. I bet John Smith and John Sutherland would do it. I saw them a little while ago, over by the corral. Bowie, you go ask them. I'll tell the sentry that if he sees them coming back any faster than a walk, to ring the bell. That will mean the enemy is really here."

The men went about their business, and soon the town was into its everyday routine. The time passed and many forgot about the earlier alarm. Colonel Travis was in his office writing a letter when suddenly the bell rang out once again. Travis grabbed his sword and ran to the bell tower. He got to the top just behind Bowie.

They rushed to the sentry and looked to where he was pointing. They could see two men riding their horses as fast as they could toward town. "That's Smith and Sutherland," Bowie called. "They sure must have seen something. Look at them ride."

Travis and Bowie raced down the stairs. They were waiting as the two scouts pulled their horses to a stop. "What did you see?" Travis asked.

The men had to catch their breath before they could answer. John Smith pointed down the road. "Soldiers. Lots of them. I have never seen so many."

"What were they doing?" Bowie asked.

Sutherland wiped his forehead with his sleeve. "They were sitting in a dry wash. It seems they are waiting for something."

"I bet they're waiting for the rest of the army. This is probably just the first part of the army. The rest can't be far behind," Bowie said.

Travis nodded. "I think you're right. We need to pass the word to everyone to get into the Alamo before Santa Anna gets here."

Before long, the word of Santa Anna's army being outside of town had spread. Everywhere men were grabbing their possessions and heading toward the Alamo.

Susannah looked up as Almeron rushed into their house. "Almeron, what's happening?" she asked.

"Quick," Almeron said. "Don't ask any questions. Give me the baby and climb on the back of my horse. Santa Anna is here, and we must get into the Alamo."

The streets were crowded with people. Some were rushing toward the Alamo. Some were hurrying out of town. Davy Crockett and his friends were heading toward the Alamo. He saw Susannah and gave her a smile. Jim Bowie and his sisters-in-law were loading a wagon with some belongings. Bowie coughed as he carried some trunks to the wagon. Travis tried to direct the people, but finally gave up and hurried to the Alamo to organize the defenses.

Some men were driving a small herd of cattle down the streets. Others carried bushels of corn they had found. This food would be needed during the coming battle.

The small bridge over the river was too crowded, so Almeron rode down to a little ford and splashed his way across to the other side. Soon, he was riding through the gates of the Alamo. He stopped his horse in front of the Alamo chapel. He jumped off the horse and took the baby as Susannah slid down from the saddle. "Come on," he said. "We'll find you a room in the chapel where you and Angelina will be safe."

Meanwhile, Santa Anna had joined General Sesma's men. He was not happy as he rode up to the general. "What are you doing here?" he asked. "Didn't I tell you to attack the Texans?"

"Yes you did, sir. But it took us longer than I thought to get here. Then I heard a bell ringing. I thought the Texans were going to attack me, so I hid in this wash until I could tell what was happening."

"You thought they were going to attack you? You have over one thousand men. My reports say the Texans have less than two hundred. Why would you think they would attack you?"

General Sesma looked at the ground and said nothing. Santa Anna shrugged. "Oh well, it really doesn't matter. Now, I can lead the attack. Come on, let's go get rid of this nest of traitors."

Santa Anna rode on, and his men followed him into San Antonio, just as the last of the defenders were entering the Alamo.

# Chapter Eleven

"Lady Texas," Nancy said, "why did the Texans run into the Alamo? They could have gotten away. Now they have no chance."

Lady Texas smiled and put her arm on Nancy's shoulder. "Sometimes it's hard to understand why people do the things they do. But it usually makes sense to them. The Texans had a real belief that they must stop Santa Anna here. This would save their homes and their families from having a war come to them. Sometimes people think a thing is worth fighting for. When that happens, what they do doesn't always make sense."

Jimmy looked at the men organizing the Alamo's defenses, then he looked at Santa Anna's army marching into San Antonio. "If I had been there, I would have fought too. I wouldn't have been afraid," he said.

"I know you would have been brave like those men," Lady Texas said. "Let's hope you never have to be. Now watch, because we must be back before the museum opens."

Inside the Alamo the men were loading their rifles and running to their places on the walls. Davy Crockett knocked on Travis's door and walked in. "Colonel Travis, it seems everybody is going to their places, but my men and I don't have a spot to defend. Where would you like us to be?"

Travis looked up from his desk, where he had been writing a letter. "I think the best place for you would be on the south wall, where we built the stockade. It's not a very strong position, but it'll be stronger if you and your men defend it."

Travis returned to his letter. Crockett gave a little shake of his head and walked into the courtyard.

"Where do we set up, Davy?" one of his men asked.

Davy pointed to the wall of pointed stakes. "I reckon that fence will suit us just fine," he said. His men looked at the fence and walked over to it without talking. Once they got there, they looked over the logs at the enemy moving through the streets of San Antonio.

Davy leaned his rifle against the wall and sat with his back to the logs. "See?" he asked. "It's starting to feel like home already."

Just then, a man yelled for Colonel Travis to come to the wall. Crockett followed Travis as he ran across the courtyard. They ran up a dirt ramp and stood next to some men who were looking toward town.

"What is it?" Travis asked.

One of the men pointed to a large red flag that had been raised on the bell tower of the church where the Texan sentry had stood not long ago. A breeze caught the flag, and it flapped in the wind.

"That's not Mexico's flag," someone said. "I wonder what it means?"

Juan Seguin looked at the flag, then said, "It means that Santa Anna will show no mercy in the coming fight. He is telling us that if we want to fight him, we will all die."

The men stood in silence and watched the flag blow in the breeze. Finally, Davy Crockett spoke. "I wasn't planning to ask for any mercy. Just because Santa Anna has a big red flag, it don't mean he's going to win. I plan to have a say in who gets killed and who doesn't."

"Yeah," Green Jameson agreed. "I didn't come all the way from Kentucky to have somebody like Santa Anna tell me how things are going to be."

"That's right," someone said. "When this fight's over, Santa Anna might be wearing that flag while he runs back to Mexico."

The men laughed and cheered. They watched as a band marched into town playing loudly. The sun shone on their instruments, making them seem to glow.

"Would you look at those fancy uniforms," Crockett said. "And my, can they march. I don't believe I've seen such high-stepping since Aunt May walked barefoot through the ant bed."

The men laughed at Davy's statement. "You know," one of them said, "I think we should have that band play at our next party."

All the men agreed that would be a good idea. While they were discussing this, a messenger rode from town toward the Alamo.

"Wonder what he wants?" Travis said.

Jim Bowie watched as the rider came nearer to the Alamo. "Maybe Santa Anna wants to surrender," he said.

Soon the messenger stopped his horse in front of the wall where the men stood. He looked up at the Texans standing there and began to read a message from Santa Anna. The message told the Texans that they were greatly outnumbered. Shortly they would be surrounded, and there would be no escape. If they wanted to surrender now, then they would be treated as Santa Anna felt that such men should be treated. If they chose to fight, then they would all die. When he had finished, the messenger looked at the men, waiting for a reply.

Jim Bowie looked at the army still marching into San Antonio. "Well, Travis," Bowie said. "Do you have an answer for Santa Anna?"

Travis had been leaning on a big cannon. He stepped back and looked toward town.

"Yes, I do," he said. "Captain Dickinson, fire the cannon."

# Chapter Twelve

The men stood staring at Travis. Finally, Jim Bowie said, "Are you crazy? If you fire that cannon, we have no chance of working something out with Santa Anna."

Travis looked down at the messenger, who sat on his horse waiting for an answer. "We have no chance of working out a deal now. Did you hear what the messenger said? Santa Anna will treat us as he feels we should be treated. Do you see that red flag? There's no talking now. Captain Dickinson, I said fire the cannon."

Almeron Dickinson, Gregorio Esparza, and Tapley Holland loaded the cannon, and Dickinson held the match as he once more looked at Travis.

"Captain Dickinson, Santa Anna is waiting for our answer. We shouldn't keep him waiting any longer. Fire now."

Dickinson touched the match to the powder, and a loud explosion sent the cannonball flying toward San Antonio. The soldiers on the plaza looked up when they heard the cannon roar. They watched as the cannonball bounced down the street and rolled to a stop against the wall of a house. The messenger looked at the men standing on the wall. He turned his horse and rode back to town.

Travis watched as the soldiers in town ran to their posts. "Do you think Santa Anna understood our answer?" he asked.

"I think he understood the answer," Juan Seguin said as he watched the enemy soldiers load their cannon. "But I don't think he liked it."

"All men, get to your posts," Travis said. "Ladies, you'd better get to your room. There are going to be a lot of cannonballs flying around here real soon."

The enemy cannon began to pound the walls of the Alamo. Some of the cannonballs fell into the courtyard and threw up showers of dirt when they exploded. The men ducked behind the walls to escape the flying metal.

Inside the chapel, the women sat in their small room and listened to the cannonballs crash against the walls. Now and then, they could hear a man's voice yelling, but they could not understand what was being said. It was dark in their room, but when the Alamo cannons fired, the flash gave them some light.

At last the firing slowed down. Susannah held her daughter as she leaned against the wall. Ana Esparza,

Gregorio's wife, sat next to her. "It seems like the firing is stopping," Ana said.

"Yes," Susannah said. "Ana, did Gregorio try to get you to leave San Antonio?"

"Oh, yes. Many times. He told me I should go where it's safe. I could have gone to a friend's ranch, but I believe that my place is with Gregorio. We are a family. My children and I won't run away just because there's danger."

"How many children do you have, Ana?" Susannah asked.

"I have four. Three boys and a girl. One of the boys is named after Gregorio's brother, Francisco. It's sad. Francisco is in Santa Anna's army. He is out there right now. He might be shooting the cannon at us."

"Listen. It sounds like the cannon are starting to fire again," Susannah said. "I hope they stop soon."

The cannons didn't stop; they fired all night long. The men couldn't sleep because of the cannon fire. Santa Anna's band played loud music to help keep the Texans awake.

When the sun rose the next day, everyone was glad to see that, in spite of all the cannonballs flying into the Alamo, no one had been injured. The Texans were in a good mood as they walked out into the early morning sunlight. They had survived.

Colonel Travis was talking to James Bonham as they walked through the open courtyard. "We have to send some messages to the government. They need to know that Santa Anna is here. They need to send us more men and supplies right away."

"I'll go," Bonham said. "Give me the letter. I'll find the government and get them moving."

Travis shook his head. "No, I have another job for you. I want you to go to Colonel Fannin at Goliad. He has the biggest army in Texas. Get him to send us at least part of that army. I'm sure he'll come as soon as he hears what's going on here."

"We better get going soon. I bet Santa Anna's going to surround this place soon. That'll make it a lot harder to get out."

"I nearly have your message ready. I need to work some more on the one to the government. I need them to understand how badly we need more men."

Bonham laughed. "You have a way with words, Bill. I bet you come up with something real good."

Men were cooking their breakfast over open fires, and the smell of roasting meat made Travis and Bonham hungry. They stopped by a campfire and cut a slice of meat as it slowly turned over the fire. It tasted good, and they stayed by the fire and talked to the men who were there for a while.

They looked up and saw someone running toward them. As the figure got closer, they could tell that it was Juana Alsbury, one of Jim Bowie's sisters-in-law. She ran up to Travis and stopped to catch her breath.

"What's the matter, Juana?" Travis asked.

"Colonel Travis," she gasped. "Come quick. It's Jim. He is very sick."

# Chapter Thirteen

Nancy, Jimmy, and Lady Texas stood in a corner of the room and watched as Travis followed Juana Alsbury into the room. Her sister, Gertrudis Navarro, was kneeling by the bed, wiping Bowie's forehead with a damp cloth.

"What happened?" Travis asked.

"He was getting ready to go outside when he started to cough and then he fell on the floor. All I know is that he is very sick," Juana said.

"Have you sent for Dr. Pollard?" Travis asked.

"Yes," Juana said. "We sent someone quite some time ago. The doctor should be here any time."

Travis looked at Bowie, who tossed on his bed. "I told him to see a doctor some time ago. I knew this cough was more than just a cold."

Everyone looked up as the door opened, and Dr. Amos Pollard walked in. He walked over and looked at Bowie. He reached into his bag and took out a small bottle of medicine. He put some in a cup and lifted Bowie's head and had him drink the medicine.

When Bowie was finished, he laid his head down and stood up. He turned to Juana and Gertrudis. "Make sure you keep him warm. I'm going to leave this medicine with you. Give it to him when he starts to cough. Wiping his head with those wet cloths is a good idea. I'll check on him from time to time."

"What's wrong with him, Doctor?" Juana asked.

Pollard wiped his forehead with his sleeve. "I can't say for sure. It's tuberculosis, pneumonia, or some other kind of consumption. The only thing I know for sure is that he is very sick. I need to go check on some other men. I'll be back soon."

"Lady Texas," Nancy said. "What will happen to Jim? They don't have the medicines we have now. I wish I could take him to the hospital."

"They will do the best they can," Lady Texas said. "Everyone must do the best they can with what they have. People throughout history have done that. It's important for us to learn from the past, so we can make our lives today better."

Jimmy nodded. "I'm beginning to see that now. When I get home, I'm going to pay more attention in history class."

Lady Texas smiled. "Good for you, Jimmy. Now let's see what happens."

"I must go now, too," Travis said. "I need to send out some messengers to tell the settlers that Santa Anna has arrived. I'll check on you later."

Travis walked outside. He leaned against the wall and closed his eyes. They couldn't afford to lose any men, and certainly not a man like Jim Bowie. Maybe he would get better. Travis hoped so. But right now he had to get the messengers on their way.

He entered his room and sat at his small desk. He took out paper and a pen and thought about what he wanted to say. The people had to understand that the Alamo needed more men. And they needed them soon. Finally, he took his pen and began to write.

*Commandancy of the Alamo*
*Bexar, Feby 24th, 1836*

*To the People of Texas and all Americans in the World—fellow Citizens and Compatriots:*

*I am besieged with a thousand or more of the Enemy under Santa Anna. I have sustained a considerable bombardment and cannonade for twenty-four hours and have not lost a man. The enemy has demanded a surrender at discretion, otherwise the garrison is to be put to the sword, if the fort is taken. I have answered the demand with a cannon shot, and our flag still waves proudly from our walls. I shall never surrender or retreat. Then, I call on you in the name of liberty, of patriotism, and everything dear to the American character, to come to our aid with all dispatch. The enemy is receiving reinforcements daily and will no doubt increase to three or four thousand in four or five days. If this call is neglected I am determined to sustain myself as long as possible, and die like a soldier who never forgets that which is due his honor and that of his country.*

*VICTORY OR DEATH*
*William Barrett Travis*
*LT. COL. Commanding*

*P. S. The Lord is on our side. When the enemy appeared in sight we had not three bushels of corn. We have since found in deserted houses 80 or 90 bushels and got into the walls 20 or 30 heads of beeves.*

*Travis*

When he finished writing the letter, Travis read it a couple of times. He wanted to make sure he had said what he wanted to say. The people had to understand the need for more men. Finally, he was satisfied.

He put the letter and some others in a saddlebag. He walked over to the door and went outside. He walked over to one of the men standing by a horse. He handed the saddlebags to him. “Here, Albert,” Travis said. “Get these letters to the government as soon as you can. And if possible, bring some more men back with you.”

Albert Martin climbed into the saddle. “Don’t worry, Colonel,” he said. “I’ll be back before you know it.”

Travis turned to James Bonham, who was sitting on his horse. “James, you know what to tell Colonel Fannin. Get to Goliad, and bring us some men. When you come back, tie a white handkerchief around your hat. That will let us know to let you in.” Travis shook each man’s hand. “Good luck. We’ll be waiting to hear from you.”

The men rode over to the Alamo gate. The door swung open and the men galloped out. Travis listened but heard no gunfire from the enemy troops. Slowly, the horses' hoofbeats died away in the distance. Travis walked into the courtyard. There were a lot of things to do. And he would have to do them without Jim Bowie.

# Chapter Fourteen

Nancy shivered as she watched the red flag wave in the breeze. “Gosh, it’s so cold,” she said.

“Yeah,” Jimmy agreed. “It sure got cold in a hurry.”

“Yes, it did,” Lady Texas said. “That’s the way Texas is. It can be warm and sunny one minute and freezing cold the next. You can see the Alamo defenders think it’s cold too.”

The men in the Alamo were trying their best to keep warm. They ducked down behind the walls to get out of the wind. Every now and then, they would raise their heads and look over the wall to make sure the enemy was not attacking. Some of the men built fires in the courtyard and stood close to the flames, trying to get warm. The men blew on their hands as they held the metal gun barrels. At least the cold wind was keeping the enemy soldiers inside their tents. They probably would not attack in weather like this.

In his office, Colonel Travis was busy writing more letters asking for more men. Every day that passed brought more of Santa Anna's troops to San Antonio. Travis knew that the only chance the Texans had was to get more men to the Alamo as soon as possible.

He looked up as Davy Crockett entered his room. "Hello, Davy," Travis said. "How are things going?"

Crockett sat down across from Travis. He took off his hat and shook his head. "It is pretty cold for the men. We need more blankets, but there aren't any more. The men are more worried about freezing to death than about Santa Anna's troops. I can't say that I blame them. The enemy soldiers put some new cannon positions up. They are getting closer. They have been pounding the north wall so much it is starting to cave in."

Travis shook his head. "Have some men throw some dirt up there. That should help strengthen the walls. The exercise will keep them warm. I need to get more messages out right away. We can still get riders through the enemy lines, but if Santa Anna keeps getting reinforcements, we might not be able to in a few days."

"I saw some troops moving around a little while ago. They were moving toward those old shacks not far from here. I bet there's going to be an attack before long."

Travis rubbed his eyes. He hadn't slept much in the last few days. "I think we need to tear down those shacks," he said. "We could use the firewood, and it will get rid of those hiding places. Let me finish this letter, and we'll get some men together to tear down those houses."

Davy stood up to go. "All right. I'll start rounding up some men. I think it'll feel good to be out in the open air again."

Just then they heard a shout. "Look out! Here they come!"

Rifles began to fire as Crockett and Travis raced into the courtyard. They could see some men firing over the wall. As they ran to the top of the wall they could see Santa Anna's men coming out of the houses and running toward the Alamo.

"Fire the cannon!" Travis shouted.

The blast of a cannon filled the air. Smoke came out of the barrel and covered the running enemy soldiers for a few seconds. The enemy scattered as the cannonball rolled through their ranks. They ran toward the Alamo again, firing their guns as they ran. The men on the Alamo walls were cheering as they fired. Colonel Travis directed the cannon, and it fired round after round into the charging enemy. Davy Crockett ran among the defenders, cheering them on. He slapped the men on the back and yelled at the charging enemy soldiers.

The enemy finally began to move back toward the shacks. The firing died down as the enemy soldiers disappeared behind the old houses. Finally, they could be seen moving back toward the town. The defenders cheered, and some of them threw their hats in the air as they watched Santa Anna's men retreat.

Soon, it was quiet. The Texans suddenly felt tired. The battle had made them forget about the cold wind. The Texans were proud that they had driven Santa Anna's soldiers away.

Colonel Travis walked in front of the men and smiled at them. "You did a good job," he said. "I think Santa Anna was testing us to see how strong we are. He should have more respect for us now. I know it's cold out here, but we must keep watch. We don't know when Santa Anna will attack again. We must be ready at all times. Right now, we have another job to do. I need some men to go out and tear down those shacks. Who will volunteer?"

The men looked at the shacks. It was possible that there were still enemy soldiers hiding in the old buildings. It would be very dangerous to go out there. Travis began to get worried. It seemed that no one would be willing to go.

# CHAPTER FIFTEEN

THE MEN STOOD IN THEIR PLACES looking at Travis. No one moved or said anything. Nancy, Jimmy, and Lady Texas could tell that Travis was getting nervous. If the men would not do this task he was asking of them, then they might not do anything he wanted done. He knew many of the men still wanted Bowie to lead them, but Bowie was too sick to get out of his bed. This could mean the end of the Alamo defense.

"You know, I think I would like to get outside these walls for a while," Davy Crockett said. "Anybody feel like taking a little walk with me?"

"Well, Davy," Charles Despallier said. "If you're going, I guess I'll go too."

"Yeah, me too," said Robert Brown. "It's a pretty nice day for a walk."

Other men agreed to go, and soon there were enough volunteers. Travis walked up to Crockett. "Thanks, Davy. I was afraid nobody was going to go."

"I guess it shows most of these men have good sense. Now while we're out there, be sure and keep a good lookout. If the enemy soldiers attack again, you have to cover us until we can get back inside. Bowie thinks there are still some soldiers in the shacks. He might be right. You'll have to cover us."

"Don't worry, Davy," Travis said. "I'll have some men fire from the north wall. We'll make them think we are doing something there. That should take their minds off you."

"All right," Crockett said. "Well, I guess we better be going."

Lady Texas and the children watched as the Texans grabbed some torches and walked out of the gate. Some Texans started firing on the north wall. Soon, Santa Anna's men were firing back at the Texans. Davy and his men ran to the shacks and set some of them on fire. They began to tear down some others so they could carry the wood back to the Alamo.

Suddenly, several enemy soldiers ran out of a burning house. Davy and the other Texans lay on the ground behind a pile of dirt as the enemy soldiers began to shoot at them. The Texans fired back at the steadily growing number of enemy soldiers. Davy knew that soon the enemy would attack his small group.

"Where is Travis?" Davy said. He looked back at the Alamo and saw some men standing on the wall, watching the fight. "Why doesn't he cover us?"

Just then a cannon fired. The Texans ducked as the cannonball flew over their heads and landed among the enemy soldiers. The enemy soldiers ran back before another cannon could be fired.

Davy jumped to his feet. "Come on, men," he called. "Let's get out of here."

Davy began to run toward the Alamo, followed by the others. The enemy began to fire again, and rifle balls whined over the Texans' heads and kicked up dust at their feet as they headed toward the gate.

"Open the gate!" some of the men called. The gate swung open, and the men rushed inside the walls and fell to the ground, gasping for air. The men inside cheered as the Texans ran through the gate.

Davy stood up and saw Travis walking toward him.

"Good job, Davy," Travis said. "Did you lose any men?"

Davy counted the men who still lay on the ground. "No, we're all here. None of us even got hurt," Davy said.

Travis looked relieved. "That's good news. You and your men rest for a little while. I think you earned it. I'm going to my room to write some more letters. I don't know if any of my messengers got through Santa Anna's lines. We have to get more men. Real soon, too."

Davy watched Travis walk away. He walked up to the top of the wall and watched the shacks burn. At least the enemy soldiers wouldn't be able to use those for cover anymore.

Later that day, Travis, Crockett, and Juan Seguin met in Travis's office. Travis put his latest letters in a saddlebag and laid them on his desk.

"As you know, we haven't had any men join us since the battle began," he said. "We can hold out here a while longer, but we must have more men if we hope to drive Santa Anna's army out of San Antonio. I've sent other messengers, but I don't know if any of them were able to get through the enemy lines and reach the settlements. I need to send someone who can speak Spanish and who knows this country. I think that person would have a better chance of making it through."

Juan Seguin nodded. "I think that's a good idea. I have several men who could deliver the messages for you. I'll see who wants to go."

Travis stood up and lifted the saddlebags off his desk. "No, Juan. I don't want one of your men to go. I want you to carry the messages."

"Me?" Juan shook his head. "I can't go. I brought a company of men into the Alamo. I can't go and leave them. I'll send somebody else."

"It has to be you, Juan," Travis said. "You and your father are well known by the government. They would listen to you better than to one of your men. I'm not asking you to leave your men. I want you to come back, leading more men. That's the only way we can win. I know your men understand that."

"Even if I wanted to," Seguin said, "my horse is lame. I can't ride him. Send somebody else."

Davy Crockett walked over to Seguin. "Jim Bowie has a good horse. He's not going to be using him for a while. I bet he'll let you use him."

"All right," Seguin said. "Let's go see Bowie."

Bowie agreed to let Seguin use his horse. Soon, Travis, Seguin, and Crockett were standing by the gate. Seguin mounted the horses and took the saddlebags from Travis.

"I think the Gonzales road is still open," Travis said. "Try that first. There should be some men in Gonzales who'll join us."

"All right," Juan said. "I'll be back as soon as I can."

The gate opened and Seguin guided his horse out into the open road. Inside the Alamo, Travis and the others listened to the sound of the horse's hooves fade into the night. They all felt very alone.

Seguin rode his horse down the road, watching for Santa Anna's soldiers. The night was dark, and he couldn't see very far in the darkness. Suddenly, a campfire blazed right in front of him. Before he could ride away, he heard the sound of rifles being cocked.

"Who's there?" a voice called out.

"I'm a rancher. I've been out looking for stray cattle. I got lost in the dark and I'm trying to get home," Seguin said.

"Ride into the light so we can see you," the voice said.

Seguin rode slowly into the campfire's light. As he got near, he could see the rifles of the soldiers pointed right at him.

# Chapter Sixteen

JUAN RODE INTO THE LIGHT. HE held his hands where the soldiers could see them. He smiled at the soldiers as he stopped next to the fire. “This fire feels good. It has been very cold today. I have been looking for my cattle all day. I never did find them.”

“Maybe the Texans got them,” one of the soldiers said.

Juan shrugged. “Maybe. If they did, I’m not going into the Alamo to get them back.”

The soldiers laughed and lowered their guns. They sat down around the fire and tried to get warm.

"Get off your horse," one of the soldiers said. "Visit with us awhile. We never hear what's going on outside this little post."

"That fire looks real warm," Juan said as he watched the soldiers lay their rifles on the ground. When he was sure that the soldiers were not paying attention to him, Juan stuck his spurs into his horse's side. The horse leaped over the fire and ran into the night. Juan could hear the men shouting, and then he heard rifles firing. He lay low on his horse's neck as rifle balls whizzed over his head.

He rode for several miles, then he pulled his horse into some brush and listened for the sound of enemy horses chasing him. He could hear nothing but the breathing of his horse. After waiting for several minutes, Juan guided his horse out onto the road and rode into the night, eager to find the government, deliver his message, and get back to his friends in the Alamo.

Back in the Alamo, Susannah Dickinson rocked her baby as she sat in her small room in the Alamo chapel. She could hear the wind blowing outside, but the thick walls of the chapel blocked the wind from her room. She could hear Almeron and the other men talking as they kept watch on the cannon platform just outside her room. Whenever the men fired the cannon, the flash lit up her room. The smoke would drift down and fill the small space, making it hard to breathe. Her little daughter, Angelina, was sleeping. Susannah laid her on some blankets and covered her with another. She walked over to Ana Esparza, who was watching her children.

"Ana," Susannah said. "I'm going to go outside for a little while. Would you mind watching Angelina? I think she'll sleep for a while if the guns don't start firing."

"I don't mind, Susannah," Ana said. "Take all the time you want. She'll be fine."

Susannah walked to the bottom of the ramp that led to the cannon platform and called out, "Almeron, can you come down here for a minute?"

Soon, she saw Almeron walking down the ramp toward her. "What's the matter, Susannah?" he asked. "Is something wrong with Angelina?"

Susannah smiled. "No. She's fine. I just wanted to spend some time with you. It seems we haven't had much time together lately."

"I know," Almeron said. "There has been a lot going on lately."

From the enemy camp they could hear the sound of a band playing. The music was loud.

"Why is that band playing so loud?" Susannah asked. "Can't they hear very well?"

Almeron shook his head. "That music is not for Santa Anna's men. It's for us. They want us to stay awake, so they add music to their cannon fire."

"I wonder what the name of that tune is," Susannah said. "It has a lovely melody."

Almeron listened for a minute and then said, "It's called the Deguello. It's an old Spanish song they got from the Moors long ago. It means 'to slit the throat.' It is to remind us of the red flag. Santa Anna doesn't want us to forget what he plans for us."

Susannah shuddered and stood closer to Almeron. He put his arms around her, and they stood silently in the old chapel for a few minutes. Finally Almeron said, "Let's go outside. I want to see what the men are doing tonight."

As they walked into the courtyard, Susannah and Almeron saw groups of men huddled around campfires talking softly to each other. The men were tired, and they seemed sad as they talked about their homes and their families.

"What are you two doing out here in the cold air?"

Susannah jumped at the unexpected voice. She turned and then smiled as she saw Davy Crockett walking toward them. "I wanted to come outside for a little while," she said. "That room is awfully small."

"I don't blame you," Davy said. "I think this whole place is too small. I would rather be out on the prairies having Santa Anna trying to catch me, than sitting here like a bear trapped in a cave."

Susannah looked at the men. "Davy," she said, "These men seem awful sad. I wish there was some way to get their minds off of the cannonballs and the loud band. Maybe if we had our own band, we could play happy music, and that would cheer them up."

Almeron shook his head. "Well, we don't have a band. I don't see that there's anything we can do about it."

"No, we don't have a band," Davy agreed. "I know one thing that will cheer us all up. Once Juan Seguin and those other messengers get to Houston and Fannin and the others and bring back more men, we'll all feel better."

Susannah put her arm through Almeron's and looked at the main gate. "I sure wish I could see a bunch of men riding through that gate right now. Do you really think that any of the messengers got through Santa Anna's lines, Davy?" she asked.

Davy smiled at her and nodded. "Sure. I bet they all got through. I bet you right now there are hundreds of men riding as fast as they can to get here. Why, pretty soon there'll be so many men we'll have to borrow tents from Santa Anna to have a place for them to stay. Now you better get back inside where it's not so cold. Kiss that little girl for me."

"All right, Davy," Susannah said. "I'll see you tomorrow. Thanks for making me feel better."

Davy watched as Almeron and Susannah walked into the chapel. "Glad you feel better. I sure wish I did." He walked over to the palisade and stared out into the darkness, trying to see men riding through the night coming to the aid of the Alamo.

# CHAPTER SEVENTEEN

TRAVIS AND CROCKETT JOINED SOME OTHER men who gazed out over the wall, looking at the newest cannon position made by Santa Anna's soldiers. It was much closer than any of the others. The cannonballs from that cannon would be able to do a great deal of damage to the weak Alamo walls.

Suddenly, there was the sound of cheering in the plaza. The men watched as a large group of enemy soldiers marched into San Antonio. The enemy band played loud music to welcome the new troops.

"Davy, things are not looking too good for us right now. Each day the cannons move closer. Now with the new troops, Santa Anna can tighten his ring around us. It will make it harder for our messengers to get out, and for any reinforcements to get in."

"As long as we're here, we're giving Houston and the others time to raise an army. I don't know why Santa Anna doesn't send some of those men into the settlements. By the time he decides to do that, there should be a large army ready to deal with him and to come get us out of this mess."

"You're right, Davy," Travis said. "Let's go see Bowie. He might have some ideas about what we should do."

Travis and Crockett walked down off the wall. The men who remained watched silently as the new enemy soldiers filled the plaza. As the number of enemy soldiers grew, the hopes of the watching Texans sank.

Nancy turned to Lady Texas. "Why don't more men come to help Travis and the others?" she asked.

"We'll see soon," Lady Texas said. "Right now, let's go see what Santa Anna has to say."

The children followed Lady Texas into a large home, where Santa Anna was sitting at a table talking to some of his generals.

"Your Excellency," one of the generals said. "We have enough men now. Why don't we leave some here to keep the rebels in the Alamo while we take the rest and move on to attack the settlements before the Texans have the chance to raise an army to fight us?"

Santa Anna stared at the general. "General Castrillon," Santa Anna said. "The Alamo is important not only for military reasons, but it is a blot on the honor of Mexico that theses rebels took this place from my army and drove them out of Texas. That disgrace must be avenged. We must retake the Alamo, and the Texans must be sent a message about what awaits them if they choose to fight us. We are nearly ready to attack. I tell you again, when we do, I want no survivors among those fighting us. They are not soldiers. They are no better than pirates and deserve to be treated as such. I tell you once again. In this war, there will be no prisoners. Do you all understand?"

All of the generals nodded their heads.

"Good," Santa Anna said. "Now, I want no more talk about leaving here until the Alamo has been taken and the men defending it have all been destroyed. Now let's discuss the best place to put the men who have just arrived."

"What happened to the messengers?" Jimmy asked. "Didn't any of them make it through the enemy lines?"

"Come on, children," Lady Texas said. "Let's go see."

The children followed Lady Texas to a room in a small house, where Juan Seguin was talking to Sam Houston.

"As you can see, General Houston, things are very bad at the Alamo. They are getting worse every day. You need to go there at once and bring as many men as you can."

Houston laid the message he had been reading down on the table. "I know things are bad at the Alamo. I never meant to defend that old mission. I told Bowie to blow that place up and bring the cannons to me. We cannot afford to have our men bottled up in forts. We don't have the strength to fight that kind of war. We must be able to move and to pick the time and the place of our fights. Look around you, Juan. I don't have enough men to go to the aid of the Alamo. The men I do have need to be trained. They're not an army right now. When we fight Santa Anna, we must win, because we're not going to have many opportunities to beat him."

Juan took a deep breath. He was very disappointed at Houston's words. It seemed the Alamo defenders could expect no aid from Houston.

"Should I tell Travis you're not going to send any men?" Juan asked.

Houston shook his head. "You're not going to tell him anything. You're going to stay here. I need you to help me raise an army. You are going to get some of the local people to join us. You're well known around here. People will listen to you. I need you to scout for me. Keep me informed about Santa Anna's location once he begins to move. You can be of greater service to Texas doing that than going back to the Alamo."

"No, General Houston," Juan said. "I must go back. I left men there who I brought into the Alamo. I told them I would return to them. I can't stay here and abandon them."

Houston stood up and spoke quietly to Seguin. "I know how you feel, Juan," he said. "I have friends in the Alamo too. Those men are buying us valuable time. We must take advantage of what they're doing for us. I pray we can be ready to march to their aid in time. But if we can't, we must be ready to take advantage of their sacrifice. Can I count on you, Juan?"

Juan slowly nodded his head. "I will see how fast I can get some men to join us. I know what you are saying is true. But I intend to keep my promise and return to my friends in the Alamo."

"Good." Houston smiled and sat back down. "Now, I need to write the government about sending us some money to buy supplies. I'll talk to you later."

Juan walked outside. He faced toward San Antonio. In his mind he could see the faces of his friends trapped inside the Alamo. He took off his hat and felt the breeze blow through his hair.

"Hold on, my friends," he said. "I promise, I will come back to you."

# Chapter Eighteen

The days passed slowly for the men inside the Alamo. The enemy cannons fired constantly. The men had to be ready to dodge a cannonball at any time. So far, the enemy cannons had not caused any damage, except to knock some holes in the north wall. The men worked constantly to repair and strengthen the walls. No men had been injured yet. Maybe more men would come soon.

The weather was cold. The north wind swept across the open prairie and chilled the men as they huddled by their small fires or stood watch on the walls, blowing on their hands to warm them as they looked for signs of an enemy attack or for approaching reinforcements.

Susannah Dickinson and her husband, Almeron, stood against a wall in the courtyard trying to get out of the wind. They watched the men sitting around the fires. "Almeron," Susannah said. "The men look so tired. I know they can't sleep at night because of the cannons and the band. This cold weather makes it hard to rest too. I wish there was a way to get their minds off the weather and the cannons for a while."

"We're all tired, Susannah," Almeron said. "Sitting here waiting for something to happen wears a person out. I watch their faces when they are on guard duty. They watch for more men, and when they don't see any coming, they look so sad. I don't know what to do. I don't think anybody does."

"What are you doing out in this cold weather? I thought you were smarter than that." Davy Crockett laughed as he walked over to Susannah and Almeron.

"Hello, Davy," Susannah said. "I wanted a little fresh air. It gets so stuffy in that little room."

"I understand that," Davy said. "I feel a little cramped in this old mission. I still think we should have made Santa Anna chase us all over the prairies. Instead we've gone and put ourselves in a nice little box for him."

"Well, Davy, you know we all said San Antonio was where we had to stop Santa Anna. We've kept him here for a while. I'm sure Houston and others are raising an army, and they'll be here before too long."

"Maybe so. Maybe so." Davy looked around the courtyard. "You know, I think you're right. We need to come up with something to cheer the men up. It seems to me that when you're not feeling too happy, the best thing to make you feel better is some good music."

"That's right, Davy," Susannah said. "But I don't know where you'll get any good music around here. That band's music is awful."

"True enough. Those fellows can't play for anything. But I know where we can get some good music right here. I play the fiddle as good as the next man, and John McGregor thinks he can play the bagpipes really good. So, I guess what we need is a contest to see which one of us can play the loudest. I bet that will get the men to going again."

"That sounds like a great idea," Susannah said. "But if you're going to have a contest, who's going to judge it?"

"I know who," Davy said. "Jim Bowie has been lying in that room a long time. I bet he's like you and would like to come outside and get some fresh air. I'll ask him to judge it. There's John McGregor right now. Hey! John McGregor."

John McGregor walked over. "Hello, Davy. Susannah, Almeron. What do you want?"

Davy grinned. "Well now, John, I think I can play my fiddle better than you can play your bagpipes. What do you say we have a little contest? We'll get Jim Bowie to judge it. The men will like it. Might make them forget the cold. What do you say?"

"I say it sounds like a fine idea. When do you want to have the contest?"

"Well," Davy said. "I need to get Bowie to agree, but that shouldn't be too hard. How about in one hour in the middle of the courtyard? Spread the word. We want as many people there as possible."

Word of the contest spread rapidly through the Alamo. By the time the contest was ready to begin, everyone who was not on guard duty was standing in the middle of the courtyard. The women had come out of their rooms and were standing with the men waiting for the music to begin. Several men carried Jim Bowie's bed out and sat him down in front of the crowd. Davy and John McGregor stood next to Bowie, each man holding his musical instrument. Bowie coughed, then raised himself onto his elbows and spoke.

"All right. Let's get this party started. The rules are, there are no rules. Just play what you want. I'll try to see if I can tell anything about what you're playing. Let's go."

John and Davy raised their instruments and began to play. At first it was just a bunch of noise, but slowly a tune began to develop, and soon the defenders were clapping to the beat of a song. Almeron and Susannah began to dance. More men asked ladies to dance, and before long the courtyard was full of Alamo defenders happily stomping away to the loud music. The music got faster, and the dancers tried their best to keep up. When the music stopped, the dancers cheered and called for more. After several tunes the defenders and ladies were too tired to dance anymore. They stood around Davy and John and clapped and cheered.

"Well," Jim Bowie said. "I think it's time to get out of the cold. We better end the party."

"Wait a minute, Jim," Davy said. "Who won the contest?"

Bowie shook his head. "That was so bad I couldn't tell who won. The only thing I can think to do is have another one sometime, and maybe I can pick a winner then."

The men cheered and agreed another contest was called for. The men walked back to their posts and the ladies returned to their rooms. They all felt better now.

Davy walked with Susannah and Almeron toward the chapel. Suddenly he stopped. "Listen. Do you hear that?" Davy asked.

"I don't hear anything," Susannah said.

"That's right. No cannons. No band. It's nice and quiet."

"I guess Santa Anna wanted to listen to you too," Almeron said.

"Well, I might have to change my opinion of him. He must be a person who enjoys good music. I bet he has us go over and teach his band how to play. Well, let's get out of this wind."

# CHAPTER NINETEEN

"WHY DON'T OTHER PEOPLE COME?" NANCY asked.

"Yeah," Jimmy said. "I thought Sam Houston for sure would have come before now. Colonel Travis has sent out a lot of messages. It seems like somebody would have answered him."

Lady Texas smiled and put out her hands. "Come on. Take my hands. We'll take a little trip and see what's going on."

"Where are we going?" Nancy asked.

"We're going to Gonzales. It's where the war really started. There are people there who want to help out. Come along."

Soon, the children and Lady Texas were standing in a crowded room in a little building in Gonzales. The room was filled with citizens who were talking about the Alamo.

"All right," John King said. "Don't everybody talk at once. You'll all get your say. Albert Martin, what do you have to say?"

The room grew silent as Albert Martin rose. He took off his hat and rubbed his head. Finally, he looked at the crowd in the room.

"When I left the Alamo a few days ago, they were in bad need of men. Santa Anna's army was marching into town, and I could see they had a lot more men than Travis and Bowie. Colonel Travis told me to round up as many men as I could and get back to the Alamo real fast. I'm sure that Santa Anna has had more men come to San Antonio. I'm not so sure about more men coming to join Colonel Travis. I know he was going to send messages to Houston and Fannin. I hope they're on their way. All I really know is that we need to send some men right away."

A hum of talking began when the men heard those words.

"Let's wait for Houston. He should be coming through here soon. We can join up with him and go aid the Alamo," one man said.

John W. Smith stood up. He was a well-known scout, and the men respected his opinion. "I imagine that Houston will come here someday. The problem is, Travis needs men now. If we can send some, it will help him hold out until Houston and the others can get there. I say let's go on now. Houston and Fannin can come later. I bet Fannin is already coming. He has the most men at Goliad. He's probably already on his way. We can meet up with him and go to the Alamo together."

"I don't know," one man said. "If we go off by ourselves, we might not have enough men to get through Santa Anna's lines. I think we need to wait."

Jacob Darst stood up. "Do you remember last fall when General Cos sent men to take back the cannon the Mexicans had given us? When we sent out word we needed more men, lots of folks came to help us fight. Now, Travis is asking us to come help him fight. We need to go help him like those men came to help us last fall. I feel sure more men will come. I say we need to go now."

"What about our families if we all leave? What will happen to them?" somebody called out.

John King raised his hand for silence. "It appears that we have a difference of opinion about what we should do. I think we need to leave this up to each man. You do what you think is best. I will go to the Alamo. If you want to wait for Houston or stay and protect your families, then that is your choice. Who will go with me to San Antonio?"

Some men walked to the front of the room and stood next to King. Albert Martin, John W. Smith, and Jacob Darst were among the first to join him. Slowly, others came and stood beside him. Isaac Millsaps stepped forward with the others.

"Isaac, maybe you better stay here," King said.

"Why's that, John?" Millsaps asked.

"Isaac, your wife's blind, and you have seven children. Maybe you should just stay here and take care of them."

Isaac looked out over the room at the men still sitting at their tables. "There are plenty of men who are staying here. Some of them can look after my family for me. I believe I have as much right as anybody else to go fight Santa Anna. That's the best thing I can do for my family."

One man in the back stood up. "I'll look after them, Isaac."

Millsaps smiled at the man. "Thank you. I know they'll be in good hands."

King looked down the line of men standing next to him. He counted to himself. "Looks like we have thirty-two men willing to go. Go on home, say your goodbyes and get some food to take along. We'll meet back here in one hour."

The men left the meeting and went to their houses. They said goodbye to their families and rejoined the others who were going to the Alamo. They slowly rode out of town, each man thinking about what he was leaving behind and what he was riding into.

As they rode past John King's house, William King, John's fifteen-year-old son, ran out and stopped the group.

"What do you want, William?" his father asked.

"You need to stay here. Mother and the other children need you."

"I've said I would go to the Alamo. You can watch after them."

William shook his head. "No. They need you. Let me go in your place. I can fight. It will be better for everyone if you let me go."

King looked at the other men. He didn't know what to say.

Finally, Albert Martin said, "John, go on and stay. William will do just fine. You're needed here."

Without another word, John King got down from his horse. William mounted the horse and took the rifle from his father. "Be careful, William," John said.

"I will. I'll be back before you know it. After we've whipped Santa Anna and sent him back to Mexico."

John King watched as the thirty-two men rode away. When they had disappeared in the distance, he turned and walked into his house.

# CHAPTER TWENTY

THE COLD WIND FORCED DANIEL CLOUD to keep ducking behind the wall to try to stay warm. He was supposed to be watching for movement by Santa Anna's army, or hopefully some sign of reinforcements, but it was too cold to stay on the wall very long. The sun was setting, and before long it would be dark. That would make it almost impossible to see anything. He knew that when it got dark, the enemy band would begin to play the Deguello, and the enemy cannons would increase their firing.

He tried to remember how many days they had been inside the Alamo. It seemed like a lifetime. Like so many others in the Alamo, Daniel Cloud had thought that more men would come just as soon as they heard about Santa Anna's army being in San Antonio. Now, days after Santa

Anna's arrival, Cloud wondered if anybody would ever come.

The thirty-two men from Gonzales sat on their horses in the middle of a mesquite thicket. They were waiting for John Smith to return from his scouting mission. Smith knew the area very well, and he was trying to find a way for the group to enter the Alamo. It seemed like he had been gone for hours, but it couldn't have been that long. The sun was setting, and the men hoped the darkness would help them as they tried to get into the Alamo.

Albert Martin saw the horseman riding toward them. He cocked his rifle and made sure it was ready to fire. As he watched the approaching rider, he recognized John Smith. Albert smiled and uncocked his rifle.

"What did you find out, John?" Albert asked when Smith pulled his horse to a stop next to him.

Smith shook his head as he gazed back at the Alamo. "Santa Anna's pretty much got them surrounded. But over that way there's a little stand of trees. We can hide in there until it's good and dark. Then we stay close to the trees as long as we can. I think we can make it through the enemy lines. They're not paying attention. It's too cold. I don't think they believe anybody would be stupid enough to be out in this weather. When I give the signal, ride hard for the Alamo. There might be some patrols out, so stay together and keep quiet. Everybody ready? All right. Follow me."

The men followed John Smith into the little grove of trees. They could see the cannons firing at the Alamo. They also heard the band playing. They stayed in the trees for a while. At last, Smith gave the order to move out. The men followed him out of the trees, and as soon as everyone was in the open, they kicked their horses into a gallop and headed for the Alamo. A few soldiers fired at them, but they were too far away and riding too fast. No one was hit by the rifle balls.

On the Alamo wall, Daniel Cloud strained his eyes to see what the enemy was shooting at. He heard the sound of horses' hooves running toward the Alamo. He stared into the darkness, trying to see who was riding so fast.

Suddenly, in the darkness he saw a group of horsemen riding fast toward the Alamo. He couldn't tell who they were. He stared at the approaching figures for a few more moments, then yelled to the men standing by the gate. "Open the gate. Riders coming in."

The gate was opened, and the thirty-two men from Gonzales rode into the Alamo courtyard. They pulled their horses to a stop and dismounted as a crowd gathered around them.

"Hello, men," John Smith said as he brushed some dirt off his shirt. "We came to join the fight. Where can I find Travis or Bowie?"

One of the men pointed to a small room across the courtyard. "Bowie's in that room. He's real bad sick. I suspect Travis'll be here any minute now."

Travis came running up, followed closely by Davy Crockett. He looked at Smith and held out his hand. "Hello, John. Good to see you. How many men did you bring with you?"

"Colonel Travis, I brought you thirty-two of the finest men Gonzales has to offer," Smith said.

When he heard the number, Travis felt his knees buckle. “Thirty-two? Do you have any news of Colonel Fannin?”

Smith shook his head. “I thought he would be here. We didn’t see him on the way, so we thought he must have come ahead of us.”

Davy Crockett walked up to Smith and shook his hand. “Well, I bet he got a late start and he’s right behind you. I’m sure he’ll be here before long. Anyway, we’re mighty glad to see you boys. Come on, let’s hear it for these Gonzales men.”

The men cheered as Travis turned to Almeron Dickinson. “Captain Dickinson, show these men where to put their horses and get them some food. I imagine they’re hungry after their journey.”

The Gonzales men followed Almeron while the defenders went back to their posts. Soon, only Crockett and Travis were left standing in the courtyard. Travis shook his head. “I’m glad some men came, but I’m really disappointed at the number. I was hoping that many more men would have come by now. I’m beginning to think no more are coming.”

“Well, Colonel Travis,” Crockett said, “let’s don’t give up yet. These men got in tonight. Who’s to say in the next couple of days a lot more won’t be here? It takes a while to get here. It’s a big prairie out there. There could be more men coming, and these men might not have seen them. I bet there’ll be more here soon.”

“Maybe you’re right, Davy. James Bonham is talking to Fannin. If anybody can talk Fannin into coming, it will be Bonham. Yes, you’re right. I bet Bonham is leading Fannin here right now. Come on. Let’s go welcome our new men.”

# CHAPTER TWENTY-ONE

"WHERE ARE WE GOING, LADY TEXAS?" Nancy asked.

"We're going to Goliad, to the Mission La Bahia. Colonel Fannin is there with his army. James Bonham is trying to get him to bring his men to the Alamo. It is the last hope of the Alamo defenders for reinforcements."

Jimmy shook his head. "I sure hope he can talk Colonel Fannin into coming to the Alamo. I think time is running out."

James Bonham walked back and forth in front of the desk where Colonel James Fannin sat. Bonham tried to hold back the anger that was rising in him. "You mean you are not going to send men to support Colonel Travis and the men in the Alamo? They are surrounded by Santa

Anna's army. If they don't get more men soon, they will all die."

Fannin shook his head. "Like I have said before, Bonham, I can't afford to send any men. I am sorry about Travis and his men, but I have my own fort to worry about. I have received word that there is another enemy army moving up the coast. I must protect the settlers here and try and hold back that army."

"Colonel Fannin," Bonham said. "You have over four hundred men. The Alamo has less than two hundred. Surely you can spare some men to aid them in their fight."

"I'm sure that men have come from other parts of Texas. I would like to help Travis, but because of the enemy army reported in the area, my duty is to stay here. I wish I could do more."

Bonham turned and started to walk toward the door.

"Where are you going?" Fannin asked.

"I'm going to tell Travis and the others that you're not coming. They need to know no one is coming to help them."

Fannin got up from his desk and walked over to Bonham. "I'm afraid the Alamo is lost. If you go back, you will die with the others. Stay here with me. I can use a good man like you. I think we will be able to hold off the enemy army. Then we can go to the Alamo."

Bonham looked at Fannin and shook his head. "I will report the result of my mission or die in the attempt," he said.

Bonham turned and walked out of the room. He mounted his horse and rode out of the fort, headed for the Alamo.

Back in the Alamo, Travis stood on the wall and looked for signs of reinforcements. Suddenly, cheering and band music came from San Antonio. He looked at the town and saw a column of enemy troops marching into the plaza. Travis bowed his head. He had hoped for reinforcements to come to help him defend the Alamo, but other than the thirty-two men from Gonzales, the only reinforcements to arrive had been enemy troops.

He saw the plaza filling up with Santa Anna's soldiers. He looked around the Alamo at his few men. They were huddled around small fires or wrapped in blankets as they stood on the walls. They had not slept in several days. Their food was running out. The cold wind cut through their ragged clothes. Still, these men were staying to fight for Texas, and to keep Santa Anna and his army out of the settlements as long as possible.

He heard laughter coming from one of the groups that stood around a fire. He looked and saw Davy Crockett talking to the men. Crockett must be telling one of his stories again. No matter how bad things seemed, Davy Crockett could make the men laugh.

A cannon fired from the enemy lines. Travis saw the iron cannonball hit the wall and knock a chunk of it out. The constant firing had begun to weaken the walls. Every day the men spent hours repairing the damage done to the walls by the enemy cannon. So far the Texans had not lost a man. Travis wondered how long their luck would hold out.

The celebration in the plaza continued. It seemed that the line of enemy troops entering San Antonio would never end. An officer on a white horse rode into the plaza to watch the troops march by. He wore a fancy uniform, and when the men in the plaza saw him, they cheered louder. Travis realized that the officer must be Santa Anna. Davy

Crockett and some of the men came up to the walls to see what was going on.

"Well, Colonel Travis," Davy said. "Looks like we have a few more visitors."

Travis nodded. "Yes, we do. I think that's Santa Anna watching them."

Crockett looked at the officer. "He sure does dress fancy. The only thing I ever saw that looked fancier than him was a peacock in a park back East."

As the Texans watched, the officer rode out from the crowd of soldiers and rode toward the Alamo. The soldiers followed him, and soon they were looking at the old mission while the officer pointed toward the Alamo.

Davy raised his rifle and checked the powder. He held up his finger to see which way the wind was blowing. He pointed his rifle toward the officer and took aim.

"What are you doing, Davy?" Travis asked.

Davy continued to sight down the barrel of his rifle. "I'm going to ruffle the feathers of that peacock," he said.

The men watched as Davy aimed at the officer. Finally, he squeezed the trigger. The rifle ball flew toward the enemy officer. The ball took the fancy plume off of his hat. He looked toward the Alamo, then turned his horse and rode away as fast as he could. The men on the walls laughed and cheered as they watched him ride away.

"Good shot, Davy," one of them said.

"No," Davy answered. "The wind kicked up and spoiled my aim."

"Well," Travis said. "It was funny to see him run away. I think that was Santa Anna, so that makes it even better. All right, men, let's get back to your posts. If that was Santa Anna, he's going to be mad about our little joke. I think the cannons are going to be firing more than ever real soon."

The men went back to their posts. In his headquarters, an angry Santa Anna gave the word to increase the cannon fire at the Alamo.

Meanwhile, on a small hill just behind Santa Anna's lines, James Bonham was wondering how he could get through the enemy positions to give his message to Travis.

# CHAPTER TWENTY-TWO

JAMES BONHAM STARED AT THE ENEMY LINES. They were all around the Alamo. However, in some places the enemy positions didn't have many men. He selected one of these and guided his horse slowly behind the enemy position. He stayed in the mesquite to make it hard for the soldiers to see him, but none of the enemy soldiers were looking his way. A few sat around a small campfire and talked. Two or three were wrapped in blankets, sleeping on the bare ground. One man stood up and watched the cannons fire at the Alamo. The rifles were stacked several feet away from the closest soldier.

Bonham took off his hat and tied a white handkerchief around it. He took a deep breath as he put the hat back on his head. He hoped that the enemy rifles were not loaded.

Bonham kicked his horse in the ribs, and the animal leaped forward and raced toward the enemy soldiers.

The sound of the running horses made the man who was watching the cannon fire turn. He stood in silence for a few seconds. He couldn't believe what he was seeing. Why was this Texan riding into their camp?

The soldier finally shouted a warning as Bonham rode his horse through the camp. One soldier stood up in front of the horse, and the racing animal sent him tumbling through the campfire. Other soldiers began to run for their rifles as Bonham turned his horse toward the main gate of the Alamo. Bonham looked back and saw the enemy soldiers loading their rifles. He was glad that they were unloaded. Now, he believed he would make it into the Alamo.

A shout from his right made him turn his head. A troop of enemy cavalry was riding toward him. Bonham kicked his horse to try and get more speed out of the tiring animal. Some of the soldiers now had their rifles loaded, and rifle balls flew by Bonham's head. He laid low on his horse's neck to make as small a target as possible.

Bonham looked at the Alamo gate. It looked so far away. He glanced at the enemy cavalry. They were gaining on him. For the first time since he had left Colonel Fannin at Goliad, James Bonham began to believe that he might not make it to the Alamo.

"Colonel Travis," a Texan on the wall called. "A rider coming in."

Travis was in the courtyard talking to Davy Crockett when he heard the cry. He ran to the wall and climbed to the top, followed closely by Davy Crockett. They watched as Bonham rode toward the Alamo, followed by the enemy cavalry. Bonham's horse was getting tired, and the enemy was getting closer to him.

"Cover him," Travis called. "That's Jim Bonham. Open the gates."

Men on the wall began to fire at the enemy with their rifles. One of the cannons fired, and the enemy cavalry turned their horses and rode away. The men cheered as Bonham rode through the gate. His horse skidded to a stop, and Bonham leaped from the saddle. It took him a few minutes to catch his breath. Then, he walked over to Travis, who was running toward him.

"Jim," Travis said. "Good to see you. What news do you bring us?"

"I think we better go to your room," Bonham said. "I'm not sure you want everybody to hear this."

The men stood in the courtyard and watched as Travis and Bonham walked into Travis's room and shut the door. Davy Crockett turned to the men. "You boys better get back to your posts. I imagine we'll hear what Bonham has to say pretty soon."

Inside Travis's room, the men sat facing each other across the desk. "Well, Jim, when's Colonel Fannin going to be here?"

Bonham shook his head. "He's not coming."

"What do you mean, he's not coming?" Travis asked. "Doesn't he know what we're up against here?"

"He knows," Bonham said. "He says he has to defend his fort and protect the people in his area. I think he believes we're a lost cause."

"Is anybody else coming? What about Houston?"

"As far as I know, nobody else is coming. I don't know where Houston is. I don't even know if he has an army. I think Fannin has the most men right now."

Travis slumped in his chair. "I thought that when the people heard that Santa Anna was here, they would come running," Travis said. "I never thought that nobody would come to join us. You saw Santa Anna's army. They have us surrounded. We don't have enough men to hold them off when they finally attack. I don't know who to ask for more men now. I really thought that Fannin would come, or at least send some men. I don't know what to do now."

"I think the men need to be told about the news," Bonham said.

Travis nodded. "You're right. They have done everything I have asked of them. They have a right to know. Come on. We're going to get Davy Crockett and go see Jim Bowie. Maybe all of us can figure out something to do."

# CHAPTER TWENTY-THREE

NANCY, JIMMY, AND LADY TEXAS STOOD in a corner of the small room and listened as Bonham told his story to Bowie, Crockett, and Travis. When Bonham finished his report, the men were silent for a few moments. Finally, Crockett asked, "You're positive that Fannin won't at least send part of his men to join us?"

Bonham nodded. "I tried to convince him to send aid to us, but he said he must stay at Goliad and protect the people in that area."

Bowie coughed and raised himself up on his elbow. "Well, it looks like we'll have to fight Santa Anna with the men we have. So far, we've done all right."

"I guess that's what we need to talk about," Travis said. He turned to Bonham. "Jim, why don't you go find some food and rest a little. I know you have had a long ride. And don't say anything to the men about Fannin. We'll decide what we need to tell them."

The men watched as Bonham left the room. When he was gone, Travis turned to the others. "All right, what do we do now? I thought that others would be here to join us. Now we know that won't happen. What do you think we should do?"

"The way I see it," Bowie said, "we don't have a choice. You've all seen the flag. You've heard the Deguello. You know we can't give up. We have to fight as long as possible. We need to kill as many of Santa Anna's men as we can. We can hold him here a little longer and give Houston more time to raise an army. That's my opinion. Davy, you and some of your men might try and get through the enemy lines. With your skills, you might make it."

Davy smiled and shook his head. "No, I'm afraid I can't do that. If it was just old David Crockett, then I might try, but ever since that fellow wrote that play called *The Lion of the West* with the hero, Nimrod Wildfire, I've become Davy, the man who can jump the Mississippi with a wildcat under each arm, slide down a lightning bolt, and blink thunder from my eyes. People expect a lot of things from Davy. I'm trapped not only by Santa Anna's army, but by Davy and Nimrod Wildfire."

Travis looked at Bowie. "How about you, Jim? Since you're so sick, we might get Santa Anna to let you leave. You really haven't been able to fight. He might let you go."

Bowie coughed and shook his head. "No. The way I look at it, I'm not going to live much longer either way. I don't guess it really matters what gets me, the consumption or Santa Anna. I think I'll just stay here and see this out."

Travis nodded. "All right, what do we tell the men?"

Crockett smiled. "This might sound funny coming from an old politician, but I think you should tell them the truth. These men have done everything they have been asked to do. I think they need to know the truth."

"That's right," Bowie said. "Just tell them what Bonham told us. You're good with words, Travis. You'll know what to tell them. Just have some men carry me outside. I want to listen to you."

"All right," Travis said. "I'll have the men gather in the courtyard. I think you're right. These men deserve to know the truth."

In a short period of time, Travis stood in front of the men in the Alamo courtyard. The enemy cannons had stopped firing, and an eerie silence filled the air. Travis looked at the men for a few moments and then began to speak.

"Men, I have called you here today to tell you some bad news. I have deceived you by telling you that more men were coming to join us. But I was also deceived, because I believed that more men would come as soon as they knew that Santa Anna was here. Today, Jim Bonham has told me that Colonel Fannin is not coming, and as far as he knows, nobody else is on the way. We will have to fight Santa Anna alone.

"As long as we keep Santa Anna's army here, we are giving Houston and others time to raise an army to fight him. Each day, each hour, each minute we delay Santa Anna's advance into the settlements is another day, another hour, another minute in the life of Texas. My choice is to fight Santa Anna as long as I have a breath of life in my body. As I have said, I shall never surrender or retreat.

"But I cannot make that decision for you. Each one of you must decide for yourselves what you will do. You have done everything anyone has asked of you. You have done all that honor and duty demand. Now, it's time for you to make a choice."

Travis walked down to the end of the line of men. He drew his sword and traced a line in the sand of the courtyard. He replaced his sword and walked back into the center of the line of men.

"If you choose to leave, you can do so now, and there will be no blame. You can try to escape through the enemy lines, and some of you might make it. If you want to surrender and throw yourself on the mercy of Santa Anna, who has shown he has no mercy, you are free to do so. If you stay here, you will surely die. But your deaths will give life to the dream we all have. The dream of a free Texas, where our families can live safe from dictators. So, now I ask for your decision. Those who wish to stay and fight with me for Texas should now cross the line."

Lady Texas, Jimmy, and Nancy looked at the line of men. They stood there staring at the line in the sand. They were thinking of their homes, their families, and their dreams. On the other side of that line, death awaited them. If they crossed the line, they knew they would never see their families again. If they left the Alamo, they might make it through the enemy lines to safety. At least by leaving they had some hope of seeing their families again. If they stayed, there was none.

"Lady Texas," Jimmy said. "I don't think anyone is going to cross the line."

# Chapter Twenty-Four

Colonel Travis looked at the men standing before him. He could tell they were thinking about what he had said. Maybe he had made a mistake in giving them a chance to leave. No, he had to be honest with them. They had done everything he had asked of them. They deserved to know the truth.

There was a movement on his right side. He turned and saw a young man named Tapley Holland walking across the line. He was hurrying, like he wanted to be the first to cross the line. He stood beside Travis and turned to face the men.

Slowly at first, and then faster and faster, the men crossed over and stood by Travis. Davy Crockett, James

Bonham, Gregorio Esparza, Almeron Dickinson, and the rest were soon across the line. They looked and saw two men on the other side of the line. One was Jim Bowie, who could not get out of his bed. The other was a man named Louis Moses Rose.

Bowie raised himself as high as he could and said, "Boys, I can't get up to join you. I would appreciate it if some of you would give me a hand in getting over that line."

Several men ran over and carried Bowie's bed across the line. The rest cheered as Bowie joined them.

Now Rose stood by himself, looking at the men on the other side of the line.

"You don't seem willing to join us, Rose," Bowie said.

Rose shook his head. "No, I don't believe I want to fight anymore," he said.

"You might as well join us, Rose," Davy Crockett said. "You can't get away."

Rose looked at the men, who were watching him carefully. He turned and looked at the wall. "I have done worse things than to climb that wall," he said.

Rose ran to the wall and picked up a bundle of his clothes. He climbed to the top of the wall and looked back at his friends. He waved at them and jumped to the other side. The men in the courtyard stood staring at the wall. Now that Rose was gone, the men felt a strong bond with the others who had chosen to stay.

Colonel Travis took a deep breath and said, "Men, I thank you, and Texas thanks you. Now, I think it's time to get back to our posts. I don't know when Santa Anna will attack, but I believe it will be soon. Captain Dickinson, I need to have a word with you."

The men walked away, and soon Travis and Dickinson stood alone in the courtyard. Travis looked around to make sure no one was listening, then said, "Captain Dickinson, as I said, I believe that Santa Anna will attack us soon. I honestly don't believe we can keep his army out of the Alamo. We don't have enough men, and the walls are not strong enough."

"I'm afraid I have to agree with you, Colonel," Dickinson said.

"I have an order for you. It is not a decision I have reached lightly. Sometimes a soldier must do things that are very difficult. I am ordering you to do such a thing when and if the time comes."

"What's the order, Colonel?" Dickinson asked.

Travis took a deep breath, then said, "When the enemy gets inside the walls and all is lost, I want you to order someone to throw a torch in the powder magazine and blow it up."

Dickinson was shocked by the order. He stood in silence for a time, then said, "Colonel, I can't do that. The women and children are in the room right next to the powder. If I blow up the powder, I'll kill all of the women and children. I'll kill my own wife and daughter."

"I know that, Captain. As I said, sometimes a soldier must do things that are very hard. Things he would never consider doing if he were not in a war. As I said, I did not reach this decision lightly. My hope is by blowing up the powder, we will kill a great number of Santa Anna's soldiers. With luck, maybe even Santa Anna himself."

Dickinson shook his head. “I don’t think I can give that order, Colonel,” he said.

Travis put his hand on Dickinson’s shoulder. “I know what I’m asking is very difficult for you. I have asked you because I have always been able to count on you. Your position is right above the powder. It will be easiest for you to have it blown up. Would you rather have your wife and child fall into the hands of Santa Anna’s soldiers? I think we know what would happen then. So, I’m asking you, Captain Dickinson, when the time comes, can I count on you to follow my order?”

Almeron stood in silence with his head bowed. A million thoughts raced through his mind as he thought about what Travis was asking him to do.

Finally, he raised his head and nodded. “When and if the time comes, and I pray it never will, I will give the order.”

Travis slapped Dickinson on the shoulder. “Good,” he said. “I knew I could count on you.”

Travis walked away, leaving Dickinson standing alone in the middle of the courtyard. He looked around and could see other men at their posts, but at the present moment he had never felt so alone in his life.

# Chapter Twenty-Five

Almeron Dickinson stood alone on the gun platform looking out at the enemy camp. His mind was spinning as he tried to decide if he could really follow Travis's order and blow up the powder magazine. For the hundredth time since he had left Travis, he prayed he would not have to make that decision.

"See anything interesting?"

The sudden sound of a voice startled Almeron, and he jumped as he turned to see Susannah standing there.

"Sorry. I didn't mean to scare you," she said.

"That's all right. I was just thinking."

Susannah walked up to him and asked, "What were you thinking about?"

"Nothing important. Nothing you would be interested in."

"Almeron Dickinson, I am interested in whatever you think about. Won't you tell me?"

Almeron shook his head. "No. Really, it was nothing."

Susannah put her arms around Almeron. "All right then, tell me what Travis wanted with you."

Almeron took a deep breath. He looked out at the enemy campfires. "Just some military stuff. What are you doing up here?"

Susannah backed away. "I came to be with you for a little while, but it seems you don't want to talk to me."

Almeron turned to her. "I do want to talk to you, Susannah. It's just that I don't want to talk about Travis right now."

"Well, I want to talk about what he told you. Who do you think I'll tell? Do you think I'll go running to Santa Anna and tell him?"

Almeron sighed. "Susannah, I'm not going to talk about it. If that's all you can talk about, I guess there's nothing more to say."

"I guess you're right. I'm sorry I bothered you." Susannah turned to walk down the ramp. Almeron turned and looked at the enemy camp. Susannah took a few steps, then stopped and turned around. She walked back to Almeron. "I can't walk off mad. Not now. Not when we don't know what tomorrow might bring. Let's talk about something else."

Almeron turned and put his arms around Susannah. "I'm sorry. I have a lot on my mind right now. I wish you and Angelina were out of here. Somewhere safe."

"I'm where I want to be. We're a family. We should be together. In good times and bad. When this war is over, we'll be glad we went through this together."

"Sure we will. It'll be fine. The government will give us some land for fighting, and maybe I'll open up a blacksmith shop again. We'll be real happy then. Well, I guess you better get back to the room. It's cold up here. Kiss Angelina for me."

Susannah hugged Almeron. "Good night. I'll see you in the morning." She turned and walked down the ramp. Almeron gazed out at the enemy campfires once more and prayed again that he would not have to obey Travis's order.

Susannah took Angelina and walked out of the small room. She stood in the church and looked at the stars that shone through the open roof. She heard someone coming and turned to see Colonel Travis walking toward her.

"Good evening, Mrs. Dickinson. I hope I'm not disturbing you."

"No, Colonel. I just brought Angelina out for some air. It gets so stuffy in that room."

"I'm sure it does," Travis said. "You have a nice family, Mrs. Dickinson. Your daughter is lovely, and your husband is a fine man and a good soldier."

Susannah smiled. "Thank you, Colonel. I understand you have a son."

Travis nodded. "Yes. His name is Charles. I left him with some friends when I came here. I miss him. When this war is over, if I survive, I will make a fine home for him.

If not, he will have the memory that his father was a man who died fighting for his country."

"I'm sure he's proud of you. When the war is over, you must bring him to visit us in our home."

"I would like that. Well, I better be going. I have much to do." Travis turned to go. He took a few steps, then turned to Susannah. He took some string from his pocket. He took off his ring and ran the string through it. "Mrs. Dickinson, would you mind if I gave this ring to your daughter?"

"That's very kind of you, Colonel, but you don't have to do that."

"It would make me feel better. I hope when she looks at it in years to come, she will think good thoughts of me."

"Of course I don't mind. I'm sure she will always treasure it."

Travis looped the string around Angelina's neck. "Well, as I said, I must go. I have many things to attend to. You should take the baby out of the cold. Good night, Mrs. Dickinson."

"Good night, Colonel." Susannah watched as Travis walked out of the chapel. She looked at the ring hanging around her daughter's neck. She held Angelina tightly and walked back into her room.

# Chapter Twenty-six

"Hello, Jim. How are you this evening?" Davy Crockett closed the door and walked over to Bowie's bed.

"Not much change. I don't think I'm ever going to get out of this bed. What a way for Jim Bowie, the great knife fighter, to go. Lying in bed."

"I brought you a couple of pistols. If they get inside the Alamo, you might need them," Crockett said as he laid the pistols next to Bowie.

"Thanks, Davy. Put my knife by me too, please. If they come in here, I want to be able to give them a warm welcome."

"I'll come back to see you tomorrow. We can have a talk about what we're going to do when this war is over. From what I've seen of Texas, this will be a real nice place to live."

"I look forward to the visit. I guess I'll try and get some sleep now. I seem to be tired all the time. See you tomorrow."

Davy walked out of the room. He stood in the courtyard looking at the stars. "I think those stars will look a lot better when I'm out of this old mission," he said as he walked to his post.

The night was quiet. Santa Anna's cannons were not firing, and the band was silent. Most of the tired defenders were sleeping. A few men stood on the walls, watching for any sign of an enemy attack and trying to stay awake.

Outside the walls of the Alamo, Santa Anna's men were not sleeping. They were moving into positions around the old mission and waiting for the signal to attack. They were cold, but they had been told they must be quiet and not move around. Soon, all the men were in their places. They waited for the signal to attack the Alamo.

Santa Anna was meeting with his generals in the house that he was using for his headquarters. He wanted to make sure that everyone understood that in this battle there would be no mercy shown toward the Texans. He considered them to be pirates, and he wanted them punished like pirates. He would send a message to the rest of Texas that if they wanted to fight him, they could expect no mercy. They would all die.

At last, the meeting ended. The generals went to their places. Santa Anna mounted his horse and rode with his staff to a place where he could watch the battle. Next to him stood a trumpeter who waited for the signal to launch the attack.

The minutes crawled by. The sky was still dark, but some light was beginning to show in the eastern sky. The men had been lying on the cold ground for hours. Finally one man could stand it no longer. He jumped to his feet and yelled, "Viva Santa Anna!"

The cry shattered the silence, and soon other men were yelling. Santa Anna was not happy about the noise. It had to be warning the Texans that something was about to happen. He signaled to the trumpeter, and soon the sounds of the charge filled the air. Hundreds of men ran toward the Alamo. Their feet pounding on the ground could be heard in the old mission.

Captain John J. Baugh was making his rounds on the Alamo walls. When he heard the shooting and the sounds of running feet, he jumped from the wall and ran toward Colonel Travis's room. When he got close to the room he yelled, "Colonel Travis, the enemy is attacking!"

Travis was asleep on his cot. He threw the blanket to the floor, grabbed his sword and shotgun, and ran to the north wall. All around him men were running to their places. The men on the walls were firing, and he could hear the yells of the charging enemy soldiers. Soon, the cannons began to fire, and their flash lit up the Alamo. Travis stopped on top of the north wall and looked at the attacking enemy. All around him men were firing as fast as they could. Travis raised his shotgun to his shoulder and prepared to fire.

Davy Crockett and his men fired at the enemy over the wooden wall they were defending. These men were good shots, and soon the charging soldiers were running back the other way. In a short period of time, they reformed and began to attack once more.

Jim Bowie lay on his bed and listened to the sounds of the battle. He felt the knife handle that lay by his side. The familiar touch made him feel better. He could tell from the sounds outside his room it would not be long before he would have to use it.

Susannah Dickinson and the other women huddled in their room and listened to the sounds of the battle. The flash from the cannons lit up their room. The smoke from the rifles and cannons filled their nostrils and burned their eyes. They wondered what was happening. Suddenly she heard someone yell, "They're running away!"

Susannah held onto her daughter and hoped that maybe the enemy had had enough and would not come back.

# CHAPTER TWENTY-SEVEN

SANTA ANNA'S MEN DID COME BACK. They charged at all sides of the Alamo and were able to get up to the walls. Jimmy and Nancy watched the battle with wide eyes. They had never seen anything like it before.

"Listen to the sound of those guns," Jimmy said. "I never heard anything so loud."

Nancy put her hands to her ears. She watched as Santa Anna's men put their ladders against the walls and started climbing upward. The Texans fired down at the climbing soldiers and pushed the ladders from the walls. It seemed that the Texans would drive the enemy away once more, but some of the soldiers climbed over the wall, and the

Texans were now attacked from all sides. Nancy and Jimmy jumped when they felt a hand touch their shoulders.

"Come on, children," Lady Texas said. "It's time to go."

"But I want to see what happens," Jimmy said.

"Me too," Nancy said. "We've seen everything up to now. Can't we see what happens now?"

"I'm afraid not. It will be morning soon, and people will be looking for you. We must get back to the storeroom. You can find out what happens by reading your history books."

Lady Texas took the children by the hand, and they were lifted up into a mist. As they were going up, they could see Travis fighting on the north wall. Jim Bowie lay in his bed, holding his pistols, with his knife lying by his side. Davy Crockett was swinging his rifle at the enemy who were trying to climb over his wall. Susannah Dickinson held her baby as she sat with the other women in their room and listened to the sounds of the battle. Then Lady Texas and the children were in the mist and they could not see the Alamo any more.

The sound of a key in the lock made Jimmy wake up. He saw Nancy sleeping on an old quilt she had found. The door opened, and he heard someone say, "This is the last room. I don't think they could have gotten in here."

Someone turned on a light, and Jimmy blinked at the bright light. He saw a museum guard enter the room, followed by Ms. Millican and his and Nancy's parents. He shook Nancy awake as the adults spotted them.

"Well, I'll be," the guard said. "They are in here. How did you get in here?"

"Never mind that. Are you two all right?" Ms. Millican asked.

"We're just fine," Nancy said. "We came in here and the door locked and we couldn't get out."

Ms. Millican hugged Nancy and Jimmy. "I should be mad at you. You know you aren't supposed to leave the tour. But I am just so glad to find you safe."

The children's parents hugged them, and then Jimmy pointed to the statue of Lady Texas. "See her? She took us to the Alamo."

Jimmy's father laughed. "Jimmy, you were dreaming. The Alamo is in San Antonio. That's a long way from here. And I don't think that statue can drive."

The adults laughed. Then Nancy said, "No. The real Alamo. We were there when Santa Anna came to attack the Alamo. We saw Colonel Travis, and Jim Bowie, and Davy Crockett, and Susannah Dickinson. We saw everything. We saw Juan Seguin ride out for more men. We saw the thirty-two men from Gonzales come to the Alamo. We saw James Bonham ride through the enemy lines to tell Travis that Colonel Fannin wasn't coming. We saw the men cross the line. We were there at the final attack."

Nancy's mother hugged her daughter. "Now, Nancy, you just had a dream. It sounds like quite a dream."

"No," Jimmy said. "It wasn't a dream. It really happened. Lady Texas came alive. She took us through some mist, and when it cleared we were there. We were really at the Alamo. Like Nancy said, we saw everything except the end of the battle. But, Ms. Millican, when I get back to school I'm going to read about that. I'm going to read about lots of things now. Now that I know that history can be interesting, I'm going to read a lot more."

"Well, I guess being locked in a museum overnight did some good," Ms. Millican said. "Maybe I should lock some more of my students in here."

"No, really," Nancy said. "It really happened. It really did."

"I'm sure it did," Nancy's mother said. "Well, I guess we better get you home. You need to get something to eat. It's a good thing this is Saturday, so you won't miss school."

"Don't worry," Nancy said. "I want to go to school now. I want to learn about things. I wish we did have school today."

"Let's go," Jimmy's dad said. "We can hear more of your story later."

"Just a minute," Jimmy said. He walked over and stood in front of Lady Texas. "Thank you. You taught me so much. I'll come back and see you soon."

Everyone left the room. The guard turned out the light. In the darkness, no one could see Lady Texas smile.

# The Alamo Defenders

| NAME | BIRTHPLACE |
| --- | --- |
| Juan Abamillo | Texas |
| Robert Allen | Virginia |
| Miles Deforrest Andross | Vermont |
| Micajah Autry | North Carolina |
| Juan A. Badillo | Texas |
| Peter James Bailey III | Kentucky |
| Isaac G. Baker | Arkansas |
| William Charles M. | Baker Missouri |
| John W. Ballentine | Pennsylvania |
| Richard W. Ballentine | Scotland |
| John J. Baugh | Virginia |
| Joseph Bayliss | Tennessee |

| | |
|---|---|
| John Blair | Tennessee |
| Samuel Blair | Tennessee |
| William Blazeby | England |
| James Butler Bonham | South Carolina |
| Daniel Bourne | England |
| James Bowie | Kentucky |
| Jesse B. Bowman | Tennessee |
| George Brown | England |
| James Brown | Pennsylvania |
| Robert Brown | Unknown |
| James Buchanan | Alabama |
| Samuel E. Burns | Ireland |
| George D. Butler | Missouri |
| John Cain | Pennsylvania |
| Robert Campbell | Tennessee |
| William R. Carey | Virginia |
| Charles Henry Clark | Missouri |
| M. B. Clark | Mississippi |
| Daniel William Cloud | Kentucky |
| Robert E. Cochran New | Hampshire |
| George Washington Cottle | Missouri |
| Henry Courtman | Germany |
| Lemuel Crawford South | Carolina |
| David Crockett | Tennessee |
| Robert Crossman | Pennsylvania |
| David P. Cummings | Pennsylvania |
| Robert Cunningham | New York |

| | |
|---|---|
| Jacob C. Darst | Kentucky |
| John Davis | Kentucky |
| Freeman H. K. Day | Unknown |
| Jerry C. Day | Missouri |
| Squire Daymon | Tennessee |
| William Dearduff | Tennessee |
| Stephen Dennison | England |
| Charles Despallier | Louisiana |
| Lewis Dewall | New York |
| Almeron Dickinson | Tennessee |
| John Henry Dillard | Tennessee |
| James R. Dimpkins | England |
| Andrew Duvalt | Ireland |
| Carlos Espalier | Texas |
| Gregorio Esparza | Texas |
| Robert Evans | Ireland |
| Samuel B. Evans | New York |
| James L. Ewing | Tennessee |
| William Keener Fauntleroy | Kentucky |
| William Fishbaugh | Unknown |
| John Flanders | Massachusetts |
| Dolphin Ward Floyd | North Carolina |
| John Hubbard Forsyth | New York |
| Antonio Fuentes | Texas |
| Galba Fuqua | Alabama |
| William Garnett | Virginia |
| James W. Garand | Louisiana |

| | |
|---|---|
| James Girad Garrett | Tennessee |
| John E. Garvin | Unknown |
| John E. Gaston | Kentucky |
| James George | Unknown |
| John C. Goodrich | Virginia |
| Albert Calvin Grimes | Georgia |
| Jose Maria Guerrero | Texas |
| James C. Gwynne | England |
| James Hannum | Pennsylvania |
| John Harris | Kentucky |
| Andrew Jackson Harrison | Tennessee |
| William B. Harrison | Ohio |
| Joseph M. Hawkins | Ireland |
| John M. Hays | Tennessee |
| Charles M. Heiskell | Tennessee |
| Patrick Henry Herndon | Virginia |
| William Daniel Hersee | England |
| Tapley Holland | Ohio |
| Samuel Holloway | Pennsylvania |
| William D. Howell | Massachusetts |
| Thomas Jackson | Ireland |
| William Daniel Jackson | Kentucky |
| Green B. Jameson | Kentucky |
| Gordon C. Jennings | Connecticut |
| Damacio Jimenes (Ximenes) | Texas |
| Lewis Johnson | Wales |
| William Johnson | Pennsylvania |

| | |
|---|---|
| John Jones | New York |
| John Benjamin Kellogg | Kentucky |
| James Kenny | Virginia |
| Andrew Kent | Kentucky |
| Joseph Kerr | Louisiana |
| George C. Kimball | Pennsylvania |
| William Phillip King | Texas |
| William Irvine Lewis | Virginia |
| William J. Lightfoot | Virginia |
| Jonathon L. Lindley | Illinois |
| William Linn | Massachusetts |
| Toribio Losoya | Texas |
| George Washington Main | Virginia |
| William T. Malone | Georgia |
| William Marshall | Tennessee |
| Albert Martin Rhode | Island |
| Edward McCafferty | Unknown |
| Jesse McCoy | Tennessee |
| William McDowell | Pennsylvania |
| James McGee | Ireland |
| John McGregor | Scotland |
| Robert McKinney | Tennessee |
| Eliel Melton | Georgia |
| Thomas R. Miller | Tennessee |
| William Mills | Tennessee |
| Isaac Millsaps | Mississippi |
| Edwin T. Mitchell | Unknown |

| | |
|---|---|
| Napoleon B. Mitchell | Unknown |
| Edward F. Mitchusson | Virginia |
| Robert B. Moore | Virginia |
| Willis A. Moore | Mississippi |
| Robert Musselman | Ohio |
| Andres Nava | Texas |
| George Neggan | South Carolina |
| Andrew M. Nelson | Tennessee |
| Edward Nelson | South Carolina |
| George Nelson | South Carolina |
| James Northcross | Virginia |
| James Nowlan | England |
| George Pagan | Unknown |
| Christopher Adam Parker | Unknown |
| William Parks | North Carolina |
| Richardson Perry | Texas |
| Amos Pollard | Massachusetts |
| John Purdy Reynolds | Pennsylvania |
| Thomas H. Roberts | Unknown |
| James Waters Robertson | Tennessee |
| Isaac Robinson | Scotland |
| James M. Rose | Ohio |
| Jackson J. Rusk | Ireland |
| Joseph Rutherford | Kentucky |
| Isaac Ryan | Louisiana |
| Mial Scurlock North | Carolina |
| Marcus L. Sewell | England |

| | |
|---|---|
| Manson Shied | Georgia |
| Cleveland Kinlock Simmons | South Carolina |
| Andrew H. Smith | Unknown |
| Charles S. Smith | Maryland |
| Joshua G. Smith | North Carolina |
| William H. Smith | Unknown |
| Richard Starr | England |
| James E. Stewart | England |
| Richard L. Stockton | New Jersey |
| A. Spain Summerlin | Tennessee |
| William E. Summers | Tennessee |
| William DePriest Sutherland | Unknown |
| Edward Taylor | Tennessee |
| George Taylor | Tennessee |
| James Taylor | Tennessee |
| William Taylor | Tennessee |
| B. Archer M. Thomas | Kentucky |
| Henry Thomas | Germany |
| Jesse G. Thompson | Arkansas |
| John W. Thompson | North Carolina |
| John M. Thurston | Pennsylvania |
| Burke Trammel | Ireland |
| William Barrett Travis | South Carolina |
| George W. Tumlinson | Missouri |
| James Tylee | New York |
| Asa Walker | Tennessee |
| Jacob Walker | Tennessee |

| | |
|---|---|
| William B. Ward | Ireland |
| Henry Warnell | Unknown |
| Joseph G. Washington | Kentucky |
| Thomas Waters | England |
| William Wells | Georgia |
| Isaac White | Alabama |
| Robert White | Unknown |
| Hiram James Williamson | Pennsylvania |
| William Wills | Unknown |
| David L. Wilson | Scotland |
| John Wilson | Pennsylvania |
| Anthony Wolfe | Unknown |
| Claiborne Wright | North Carolina |
| Charles Zanco | Denmark |
| John, a Black Freeman | |

*Find the rest of the Lonestar Legends Series*
*as well as these other fine titles from*
**Lonestar Legends Publishing** *online at:*

***www.lonestarlegends.org***

LONESTAR LEGENDS SERIES:

*DAVY CROCKETT*

*JUAN SEQUIN*

*SUSANNAH DICKINSON*

*WILLIAM B. TRAVIS*

*THE ALAMO*

OTHER TITLES:

*A BADWATER HOMECOMING*

*KING OF THE LLANO*

*TEXAS REBEL*

*THE LAST COWBOYS*